PENGUIN BOOKS

# ALEXA

Andrea Newman was born in Dover in 1938 and brought up in Shropshire and Cheshire. In 1960 she graduated from London University, where she married while still a student, and then worked as a civil servant and a teacher before becoming a full-time writer.

Her publications include *A Share of the World* (1964), *Mirage* (1965), *The Cage* (1966), *Three into Two Won't Go* (1967) and *A Bouquet of Barbed Wire* (1969), of which the last two have been published in Penguins. *A Bouquet of Barbed Wire* was recently dramatized by her as a seven-part series for London Weekend Television. She has also contributed to other television series such as *Tales of Unease, The Frighteners, Love Story, Seven Faces of Woman, Intimate Strangers* and *Helen, A Woman of Today*.

Andrea Newman is divorced and lives in London.

D1347653

ANDREA NEWMAN

# ALEXA

PENGUIN BOOKS

Penguin Books Ltd, Harmondsworth, Middlesex, England
Penguin Books, 625 Madison Avenue, New York, New York 10022, U.S.A.
Penguin Books Australia Ltd, Ringwood, Victoria, Australia
Penguin Books Canada Ltd, 41 Steelcase Road West, Markham, Ontario, Canada
Penguin Books (N.Z.) Ltd, 182–190 Wairau Road, Auckland 10, New Zealand

—

First published by Triton Books 1968
Published by Pan Books 1970
Published in Penguin Books 1976
Reprinted 1976, 1977

—

Copyright © Andrea Newman, 1968

—

Made and printed in Great Britain
by Hazell Watson & Viney Ltd,
Aylesbury, Bucks
Set in Intertype Baskerville

*'. . . a monk, when he is cloisterless*
*Is likened till a fish that is waterless.'*

Chaucer: *Prologue to*
*The Canterbury Tales*

## I

CHRISTINE looked exactly the same, only thinner. I had seen her twice in the past three years and each time I had managed to catch her pregnant. Now, as she flung open the door to me, looking pale and excited and dishevelled, I was more conscious of her miscarried flatness than I had ever been of her hopeful girth. I was actually embarrassed : seeing her like this brought back phrases from her letter, a wild, untypical mixture of hysteria and even more alarming resignation to which there had to be only one response : so here I was.

'You've come,' she said, with flattering, intense relief, and we embraced.

'Hullo, love,' I said automatically. 'Of course I have.' She smelt of children : I don't know how else to describe it. Soap and talcum and urine and disinfectant and biscuits all combined to cling to her, and to me it was the smell of children. I felt a wave of pity for her and I hugged her bony shoulders hard. Then we stepped back to inspect each other.

'How are you?' I said. 'You look fine. Do you feel awful?' And I picked up my suitcase.

She took it from me. 'You don't have to be polite,' she said. 'I look awful, I know I do, and I feel awful. You look fabulous, as usual. Do come in, you must be tired.'

Behind her, I now saw, was the two-year-old clutching at her legs, and beyond him, in the room we entered, the one-year-old in a play-pen. Both children stared at me with profound distrust, as children always do; this deepened as I flashed them my uneasy, auntish smile, not something I do well. Christine seemed not to notice. She went on talking so I mercifully did not have to pile falsehood on falsehood by clucking at them too.

'God, I'm glad to see you,' she said, dumping my case amongst the litter of toys on the floor. 'I was afraid something would happen to stop you. All day I've been thinking there'd be a telegram saying you couldn't come. I nearly went out to avoid getting it. I told you I was going round the bend; well, now do you see what I mean?' And she sank into a chair from which she first removed a plastic duck, a picture book and a bag of sweets. I cleared a corner of the sofa and sat opposite her. She frowned vaguely.

'It's chaos, isn't it?' she said. 'I know it is but I can't do anything about it. That home-help woman left last week and I'm supposed to be officially okay again but I just can't cope. Classic symptoms of inadequacy and all that. I just let things pile up round me and I sit in the wreckage and howl. The children can't understand me; I think I frighten them.' And she turned on a sudden smile that I found most alarming in its phony brightness. I was so alarmed, in fact, that I said the first stupid thing that occurred to me : 'You need a holiday,' at which idiocy the smile understandably broke into a laugh.

'Oh yes,' she said. 'Why ever didn't I think of that?' And picked up the two-year-old who was trying unsuccessfully to climb up her bare legs. He sat heavily on her lap and glowered at me with deep suspicion.

'I'm sorry,' I said. 'I mean I wish you could have one. Are you really sure you can't?'

'Not till the end of term,' she said. 'Not till Paul breaks up. And he's only just gone back.'

'I meant without Paul,' I said. 'Isn't there anyone who could look after the kids and let you get away? You could come and stay with me. It's ages since you were in London. It would be fabulous – just like old times.' And a wave of nostalgia hit me at once.

'Oh, London,' she said meditatively. 'Is it really there? Still? D'you know, sometimes I can't believe it exists at all, let alone that I used to live there. Is it just the same?'

'Yes.' We both, I noticed, used the same tone of voice, as if discussing a former lover. 'It's just the same. It's wonderful. It would do you good.'

She rocked the two-year-old with automatic tenderness and he put his thumb in his mouth. 'All noisy and dirty and wonderful,' she said slowly.

8

I nodded. 'All full of buildings and people.'

'And shops,' she said enviously. 'With clothes like yours.'

I was not wearing anything special; in fact on the King's Road I often felt I was a trifle conservative and had to remind myself that I earned my living with my brain not my thighs, but here, faced with the fact of Christine's poverty, I felt I had stepped from the pages of *Vogue* at least. I did a rough estimate of what my outfit had cost and experienced a warm glow of shame.

'Oh, it's all right,' she said quickly. 'I love it. If I can't look like that any more I'm glad someone can. It's marvellous just to look at you. I could eat everything you're wearing, starting with your shoes.'

I kicked them off. 'Try them on,' I said. We took the same size. But she frowned and said, 'Not without stockings.' This seemed to break the flow of our conversation and we sat for some time in silence while I surveyed my toes and wondered if I should put my shoes on again. Being new and the height of fashion they were uneasily poised between the beautiful and the hideous; they were also, at some later date, going to be very comfortable. Meanwhile, it was a distinct relief to get them off.

Christine went on rocking the two-year-old and the two-year-old went on sucking his thumb and the one-year-old went on rattling the beads on the bars of the play-pen. I didn't mind the pause; it gave me time to relax and think, and I enjoyed staring at Christine and reconstructing some of her former austere Madonna-like beauty from her pale face and pale hair and thin, unpainted features.

'So,' she said suddenly. 'When does your new book come out?'

For once in my life this was something I wanted to play down. In fact it would even have been a relief to be able to tell Christine that my publishers had rejected it, that I too was downhearted and miserable and my life was a mess. I felt positively guilty at arriving in a taxi and flaunting my Mary Quant suit and talking about my success. And I also felt that, however confidently I might talk, I knew that success was the most precarious of achievements and to boast

9

of success was to invoke failure, and yet to say anything along these lines would suggest a nauseating false modesty.

'Oh,' I said, 'not till next year. Spring, I think. I won't have proofs till the autumn; I've only just corrected the typescript.' I tried to be as brisk as possible and make it all sound like a necessary but rather tiresome chore. Not a beloved child gone after the others to seek its fortune, like them, in a world that might yet be hostile. I shivered at the thought and wondered, looking at Christine and her children, if this was the same protective tenderness and apprehension that she felt for them and their future. If so, and I thought it probably was, then we had more in common than either of us had guessed.

'And do they like it?' she said. 'Are they pleased with it?'

'Oh yes,' I said deprecatingly. 'I think so. Well, you know. They've accepted it. They never rave about anything till it makes money and then they tell you how they thought it was great all along.'

Christine smiled, the first really normal and relaxed expression I had seen on her face since my arrival, and it occurred to me that she wanted to envy me, that she needed my success, and that I would have been even less use to her as a failure. The idea cheered me, and as if to confirm it she said softly, 'You *have* done well, haven't you?' with real tender satisfaction in her voice.

I gave the only possible reply : 'I've been very lucky,' but I smiled too, to show the depth of my gratification, and her smile deepened.

'I'm so glad,' she said. 'It's marvellous. I can boast about you to people. And I do. It's wasted on them, most of them, but I still do it. You've made it. It's nice to know someone has.'

I looked at her hands, while wondering how to reply to this, and they were red and cracked and rough, and then I looked at the grand piano that occupied about one third of the room and saw that its lid was closed and thick with dust and scattered with various childish objects. And I was never more relieved in my life than when the baby, at some unobserved mishap, let out a wail, hesitated, and then decided to cry in real earnest.

Christine eased the two-year-old onto the floor, at which he protested, and moved to the play-pen to extricate the baby who cried all the louder for being comforted. But she moved with such slow automation that each action revealed a million similar actions that had gone before, and also a sort of mindless state in which these actions could be performed, so that children could be comforted while Christine slept or wept.

'I should be offering you a drink or something,' she said vaguely above the uproar. 'I don't know what we've got; Paul was meant to go to the off-licence last night but he didn't. He just went on marking till it was too late. Oh, I don't know,' she added, somehow managing to express an infinity of chaos and uncertainty while still cuddling and murmuring to the baby whose cries gradually ceased. 'Have a look. There may be some sherry left.'

'It doesn't matter,' I said. 'I don't specially want a drink.' But I had a look and there was some sherry left and I thought it might do us good so I poured two glasses.

Christine sat with the baby on her lap and held her glass marginally out of his reach while he did his best to upset it and the two-year-old did his best to climb back onto the coveted lap. 'Oh God,' she said presently. 'What it is to be indispensable. And in ten years I won't even be allowed to kiss them in public. Did you have a good journey?'

The sherry stung my mouth deliciously. 'It was okay. I met this funny woman. She was in service somewhere and she kept saying, "London has no interest for me, none at all. My people have a penthouse there, well, they call it a flat, but I never go there."' I made the story as vivid as I could; Christine deserved entertainment. 'She was so pathetic: terribly plain with health service glasses with those wire frames, you know, and a long nose that was somehow lumpy at the end and she had a home-knitted thing like a helmet on her head with a sort of point to it, like a gnome. And she kept boasting about her people and their country-house. I think she was only just above sub-normal, if you see what I mean. And every time I thought the conversation was over she'd lean forward and offer me another confidence like "I'm a diabetic," and I didn't know what to say.'

'You could write about her, maybe,' Christine said, rocking the baby.

'Maybe.' Normally I loathed people suggesting what I should write about but I had in fact thought that the woman might run to a short story. 'It was her afternoon off and she was going to the pictures. She was so lonely and pathetic I thought I should offer to go with her.'

'I'm lonely and pathetic too,' said Christine. 'And I can't go to the pictures. So I need you more. You did right to come here.' She smiled rather grimly. 'My need is greater.' She got up, still holding the baby; the two-year-old promptly seized her by the skirt. 'At least you meet people. Even lonely old women on trains. I don't meet anyone. But then I don't go on trains. Come to that, I don't go anywhere.'

She had taken the anecdote as an offering, as I had known she would and as I had intended it. But there was a keener note of envy in her voice than I had expected, a more strident element of self-pity, which alarmed me. Despite the letter I had not thought to see Christine quite so defeated; I remembered her as tough and capable. The deterioration made me angry and I directed my anger vaguely at life, at fertility, at marriage, at men in general and Paul in particular, but most of all at fate which had ordained Christine's lot and mine so differently and so unfairly for no reason. And I was ashamed of my good luck.

'Come on,' Christine said. 'I'll show you your room.' On the stairs she turned and grinned at me ironically. 'And it's no good saying you've caught me on a bad day. Because it's always like this.'

2

THE room looked out onto fields. It was a small, white-washed room, like the others in the cottage, with oak furniture and chintz curtains, and from the window all I could see were vast expanses of nasty brown earth and green grass stretching away to the outline of the smart new housing-development on the outskirts of the village. I stood at the window and looked out and shivered. I was terrified. All the panic I had felt as my train pulled out of the station surged back; I had known then, as the London buildings slid away and the train launched itself and me upon open country, that I was going out of my element, and I was right to be afraid. Despite the fact of Christine's flattering need and my genuine desire to see her again, I had nearly jumped off the train. It seemed to me so infinitely dangerous, so tempting of providence, to leave London for anywhere but another continent or the sea; and it was only the memory that beyond Christine lay the sea which managed to sustain me at all. Past the rows of suburban backyards we went, past the gardens and the washing, and the people doing identical things, past the allotments that for some are the only escape from routine, and on, with gathering speed, into fields.

Despite country weekends in childhood, during a period when my mother believed they were good for us, like orange juice and milk, I have always had a horror of fields. They seem to me so essentially hostile to mankind and a threat to survival : I know how little I could fend for myself if I were cast adrift. Woods and hills are equally alarming, but they have a compensating beauty; nevertheless they are part of the countryside and the countryside is alien to me. Even as a child, even while enjoying the picking of blackberries, the making of daisy chains, the collecting of conkers and nuts, I knew, with some advanced sense of my own nature, that my real life lay in London and that these country excursions were perilous. I sensed even then that I was shielded from unknown disaster by the adults around me who could with their cars and their money rescue me in time and return me to reality. And I felt that they knew it, too, for all their talk about peace and quiet, rest and relaxation. Whatever they said, they did not want to get away from it all, they wanted to get back to it, and they did. Sunday after Sunday, disguising their relief with expressions of regret but growing visibly more alive with each mile that brought them nearer to work, friends, amusements, and enjoying it all the more because they basked in a sense of duty done by our health for another week. And Peter and I sat in the back of the car listening to their conversation growing more and more animated, and I longed to tell them how unnecessary these excursions were but I did not, because I could not find the words, and because some obscure sense of justice warned me that the experience was somehow valuable, that without discovering where you are an alien, you cannot know for certain where you belong.

Now, when I emerge from country into town after any length of time I feel an almost physical relief, like finally being able to go to the lavatory. Travelling for hours along country lanes or blank motorway I am scarcely able to contain my terror. I think of death; I know I would die without the comforts of urban life. I need lipstick and wine and central heating to survive; taxis and cinemas and shops. And it is useless to tell me that these are purely financial advantages and obtainable anywhere. I know this, and I choose these examples only as a pretty way of expressing my real need, which is illogical and neurotic. I need noise and dirt and buildings and people. I need to see and hear them around me in the day in order to believe I exist, and I need to wake in the night and know they are still there and immediately accessible, in order to believe that my existence is not threatened by forces beyond my control.

So now, alone in Christine's spare-room, dressed in my absurd town clothes and looking out over Christine's fields, I felt a very real panic, and I did not tell myself to calm down or to stop being ridiculous or to pull myself together, for I am infinitely tolerant of my own weaknesses, and therefore, I think, of the weaknesses of others. Instead I actually drew the chintz curtains across the window in midafternoon, and turned my back on it, and began to unpack. And the things I unpacked were not more unsuitable and eccentric clothes, or towels or cosmetics, for these might have belonged to anyone. Instead I unpacked the typescript of my new book and the notes for the features I was working on, and I took my typewriter out of its case, and all these talismen I placed carefully and reverently on the bedside table as proofs of my own identity. And I stared at them very hard for some minutes, willing them to persuade me that I had not embarked upon a perilous adventure.

# 3

WHEN at last I went downstairs again squeals and splashes were sounding from behind the closed bathroom door, and Paul was in the living-room. His presence startled me; I had not been expecting him so soon and had rather hoped to put my feet up and consume some more sherry in peace.

'Hullo,' he said, turning round from the window where he had evidently been contemplating the overgrown garden. 'Alexa. How are you?'

'Fine,' I said, and we shook hands. The handshake gave me an odd shock : I am used at home to people who either say hullo or kiss me. Formality is not something I encounter very often. And yet there was an electric quality in the pressure of Paul's handshake, which I told myself rapidly I was imagining.

'Well,' he said, smiling at me. 'Nice to see you. I'm so glad you could come; Chris gave me the impression it was a matter of life and death to her so you can imagine how relieved I am.'

The smile was so bland and the words so hostile that I was unnerved and stimulated at the same time. I said calmly, 'It's lovely to see her again,' and perched myself on the edge of the sofa where I had sat before. Paul was taller than I remembered and when I was seated he fairly towered over me. Standing as he was in the middle of the room he presented me with a problem of vision : either to look up into his face or away at some indifferent object or pointedly at his trousers. I closed my eyes.

'Tired?' he said at once. 'Let me get you a drink.' And he put a glass of sherry into my hand without offering me a choice, since there was none to offer. Then he sat, to my relief, in the chair opposite me, and stared at me, rather fixedly. His eyes were a lot bluer than I remembered; in fact the more I looked at him the more I realized that I hardly remembered anything about him at all. Now that I came to think about it, the occasions on which we had previously met were so few and the meetings so brief that he had only registered on my memory as a vague masculine blur in Christine's life. But now I was alone with him for the first time and he was staring at me. I do not mind being stared at so I sipped my sherry and stared just as rudely back. At first it seemed merely a conventional English face, pale skin and regular features, blue eyes and curly brown hair, very classic and nondescript. A young face, all public-school and head-boy, full of self-conscious dignity. ('Now then, Jones minor, the prefects and I have decided it's our duty to punish you—'). But, looking closer, I found this effect was delightfully unbalanced by a slightly Grecian nose and a rather lush mouth, with a curve and fullness more often found on Continental men, thus giving him a touch of decadent aristocracy.

'Well,' he said presently, apparently as little embarrassed as I was by our mutual staring, 'and how's the writing going?'

Now there is something about this expression. Try as I may, I cannot convince myself that it does not contain an element of patronage, an urge to downgrade. Other people, people with no axe to grind, say, 'How's your work going?' Or 'How are you getting on?' Or 'What are you working on these days?' Or even, if heavily jocular, 'Written any good books lately?' But there is something about the expression 'the writing' that suggests a childish activity to be humoured by tolerant adults. So I gave him a lovely smile, of the sort generally reserved for photographers, and said, 'Oh, it's going very well, thank you; it keeps me off the streets.' I knew that I was really too old, at twenty-five, to play this ridiculous game but I could never resist it, if it was offered to me.

'Good,' he said steadily. 'I'm glad to hear that.' And then he played an ace. 'Let me see now, is it number four or number five, the new one?'

I had to admire him. I hope I am never too mean to give admiration when it is deserved. 'It's number three,' I said. 'That's all. Don't make me old before my time.' And I signalled his turn with my eyes above the rim of the sherry glass. He took it up at once.

'Oh, really?' he said. 'I thought you were an infant prodigy.'

I smiled politely. 'Not really,' I said. 'I couldn't afford to be. They seldom last.'

Silently, he acknowledged the point and swerved slightly. 'Well, I really thought it was more,' he said, 'from the way Chris keeps talking about you. I'm afraid I haven't actually read your books; now isn't that a shocking admission?'

I put down my empty glass on the floor. 'Not at all,' I said. 'I seldom meet anyone who has. In fact, I often wonder where all the money comes from.'

Surprisingly, he grinned at this and said in a slightly rueful, almost friendly tone, 'Well, I wish I could say the same.'

Confused by this new approach, I said nothing and watched him turning his sherry glass round and round in his hands. He had rather lovely hands with long, bony fingers and well-kept nails, and I enjoyed looking at them. In fact I got myself into quite a pleasant little reverie about masculine beauty and the importance of hands, mouths, etcetera, as objects of sensual admiration, so that I was almost startled when he suddenly said, 'Well, how do you find Chris?'

'All right,' I said promptly. 'Fine.' At least I could be honest and reassuring at once, something fairly rare : she had always looked pale and, circumstances permitting, thin, and she still did.

'Really,' he said eagerly. 'You don't think she looks ill?'

'No,' I said. 'A bit tired perhaps. But she's bound—'

'Yes.' He cut in without appearing to notice. 'She's very run down, I think. I wish she could get away but it's out of the question. She's always been so strong, it was quite a shock, her losing the baby like that.' He frowned. 'For both of us, I mean.'

'Yes, of course,' I said. 'I'm sorry.'

For another moment we were still in accord and saying what we meant; then quite suddenly he seemed to remember who I was and why I was there and how the conversation had begun. He sprang up, almost violently.

'However,' he said, 'that's that and there's no point in going on about it. I'm not being a very good host, am I? Chris specially asked me to entertain you while she bathed the kids. So how about another sherry?'

I did not like the new, brisk tone much but I agreed to the sherry and he seemed glad of something to do.

'Well,' he said, handing me my glass, 'and how's life in the swinging city?' But he did not sit down again; instead he paced up and down the small room, seeming much too tall for the oak beams of the ceiling, and shooting me the occasional sharp glance.

'Oh,' I said, 'still swinging.' It was interesting to be made so clearly aware that my presence was unwelcome. I wondered if this hostility was something doled out to all Christine's friends or reserved specially for me, in which case I should be in a way honoured. I have met it before, in husbands of friends, as if they regard me as a challenge to their masculinity, capable perhaps of castrating them at a distance by 'putting them into a book'; or as a challenge to their ordered married life, as if by my very presence I might arouse in their wives a sudden wild desire to run off and embark on a life of sin in the depraved city. It is flattering and I appreciate it, but it also amused me since most of my hours of presumed dissipation are in fact spent at the typewriter with nothing more exotic than a packet of cigarettes and a deadline to sustain me. So we talked, in a desultory and spiky way about Chelsea and fashion, and plays I had seen and he had read the reviews of, and people in the news that he seemed to expect me to know intimately, and all the time I had the impression that he was holding one kind of conversation while actually wishing for another; and I also felt that his mind was not entirely with me but that he was waiting for something to happen.

When the two-year-old rushed into the room, pink and damp and naked from his bath, I was sure that was it: the change in Paul was remarkable. There were cries of Daddy and hugs and some sort of game that consisted of chasing and picking up, putting down and running away, endlessly repeated with much hysteria until both parties were breathless, and Christine arrived in the room with the baby in her arms. And although I was quite sure that the scene was natural, in the sense that it probably occurred every night, I also felt that it was a special performance, put on with particular zest for me, the onlooker, who was also the outsider. For Paul, as he played with his son and Christine as she held the baby and watched them, seemed both to be clearly saying, even while behaving normally, 'This is it. This is real. This is love and unity and we are a family, and it is you who should envy us.' So I sat and obligingly watched them, playing my part, as we all seemed to have preordained roles to perform, and wondering why people cannot simply accept each other, why there is in all of us an urge to arouse envy rather than acceptance.

When the show at last drew to a close with promises of drinks and stories and tucking in, they both hugged and kissed their children, and as Paul relinquished the two-year-old to Christine there was an uneasy second in which I might have been supposed to kiss the children too. But I did not, being unsuited to their damp kisses and disliking displays of affection that I do not feel, and even as I said goodnight to them and smiled at them, I felt Paul looking at me and felt his satisfaction that I had proved myself as unnatural as he had hoped. But the gratification was not sufficient, he had to cap it with the exit line, or the ritual would not have been complete. 'Say goodnight to Auntie Alexa,' he said, smiling.

## 4

Much as I enjoy being regarded as a freak, however, I have to admit, though only to myself, that there are times when I long with a physical desperation, as for sex or food or sleep, to have a child. Not any old child, and not simply a child of my own, but Robert's child. It is this more than anything else that makes me afraid I may be in love with Robert. These times occur rarely – usually after we have made love and not, luckily, before, and the feeling is quite painful because I really do not see any future for Robert and me that could possibly include a child. I cannot entirely convince myself that Peter and I would have had such an idyllic childhood as bastards, even rich bastards, and having known the best it is hard to settle for less, particularly on someone else's behalf. But the question is largely academic, in any case, since Robert does not believe in marriage, and I certainly do not believe in the sort of marriage that Robert and I would be likely to have.

People are in general so sceptical about perfection, whether of childhood or marriage, that I have, on the whole, ceased to boast about my parents. The very people who constantly advocate marriage and parenthood (though perhaps as a brake on intemperate habits such as free love, continental holidays and late nights) seem outraged if I present them with an ideal which actually existed and endured. Their eyes accuse me of tampering with the facts. 'Of course, you're a writer,' I can see them thinking. 'You must be making it up.' And yet the facts of happiness are there, as simple as tragedy, which they would be pleased to believe. My parents married when my mother was eighteen and already famous for her beauty, and my father was forty-five and at the height of his editorial career, a height which did not decline until his death. Their union was romantic and improbable, and the public must have waited with pleasant anticipation for its inevitable and spectacular crash. But it survived, and the reasons for its survival outrage people still further, so these too I have ceased to explain. My mother was and is incurably promiscuous, my father sufficiently arrogant to see in this no possible threat to himself. I sometimes think – and this is probably the height of romanticism, the one man, one woman syndrome – that there was no one else in the world that my mother could have married because the quality of my father's self-confidence seems to me so rare as to be unique. And for him, despite two previous marriages, there could be no other woman, simply because there was and still is only one Alexandra Fortune.

When people say to me, 'I saw your mother on telly the other night – isn't she lovely?', I agree, but I long to say to them : You should have seen her ten years ago, and not for the bloom of youth, of which she has lost little, but for the dual radiance of a secure marriage and an adulterous love. For my mother, returning from a new man's bed, fairly blazed into her home. Loaded with flowers for the house, clothes for the children, cigars for my father, she would alight from her taxi in a cloud of scent and fur and sheer animal exhilaration that literally stopped the traffic. No road was too busy for her to cross without a pause or a second glance because the physical confidence she radiated was so strong that everything stopped for her. And the gifts were not conscience-money, as people would like to suppose, but an overflowing generosity, a shared exaltation. For the more she received, the more she had to give.

In a more conventional marriage my mother would have shrivelled and died. But without marriage, she would have drifted and circled, making aimless patterns without a focus or a sense of direction. As indeed she does now. Sometimes I have to avoid her for weeks at a time because I cannot bear her sense of loss. So when people like Paul and Christine wave their little happiness under my nose it is all I can do not to say, 'Don't bother. I've seen the real thing.'

# 5

However, once the children were in bed and asleep, the atmosphere changed completely. I have noticed this before and it is interesting to watch : the emergence of the adult after six o'clock like some rare nocturnal animal. Paul and Christine almost visibly shook off their children, with a mixture of regret and relief, though they expressed only the relief; as each toy disappeared into the cardboard toy-box and each bib and pot and bottle into the kitchen, they became more and more their other selves, the selves I remembered and could respond to. And yet not quite. It was as if they looked forward all day to the evening, when civilized talk and food and drink could be enjoyed without interruption, and then when it finally came they did not quite know what to do with it. Like a bank holiday, the evening seemed a little unreal to them and weighed on them as a time they knew they were supposed to enjoy and make the most of.

'Well,' they said, 'now we can relax,' and they smiled at me and poured the last of the sherry, but they seemed in part still upstairs with the day they had put to bed: it was more real to them than the evening. I began to feel that it was up to me to convert the evening into something viable, that they were handing it to me for this purpose as part of the contract between guest and host. 'Peace at last,' they said, but with uncertain looks on their faces.

I became energetic: hospitality like any other benefit, has to be earned. 'Yes, isn't it lovely?' I said. 'How do you manage for baby-sitters? Do you get out very often?'

Christine smiled faintly and Paul said at once, 'Not as often as Chris would like,' at which she shrugged and shook her head.

'There's only the pictures at Chelmsford,' she said. 'After all. So I'm not missing very much, am I?'

This seemed to me ominous and it was surely too soon in the evening to strike a discordant note, so I said cheerfully, though with deep misgivings, 'Well, you must make the most of me while I'm here. I'll baby-sit and you two go out.'

They both spoke at once. 'Oh no . . .', Christine said, and stopped short.

Paul said, 'What a noble offer. But I doubt if you realize quite what you're taking on.'

'Well, I'll soon learn,' I said. 'Why shouldn't I learn? It's all useful experience.'

Paul raised his eyebrows. 'Don't tell me,' he said, 'you're thinking of taking the plunge.'

It was not an expression that suited him and I was

wondering what made him use it when Christine said rather crossly, 'Oh don't be silly, darling, she means useful experience for *books*,' giving the word an emphasis that suggested life was of very secondary importance.

'Oh, of course,' he said. 'It's all grist to the mill, I suppose. Is it?'

I didn't like the sound of this much but was about to agree honestly that it was, however callous that sounded, when Christine said, 'Alexa, how's Robert? You haven't mentioned him lately.'

I had known this must arise yet I still felt my stomach overturn at the name. It's inevitable, it seems : Pavlovian almost. I should be used to it by now. 'He's fine,' I said, 'as far as I know. He's in New York.' And immediately I saw the plane taking off and myself watching behind the airport glass, amazed at my blinding tears and sudden presentiment that I would never see him again. A totally unknown man had taken pity on me and bought me brandy and turned out to be a reporter who had once worked for my father on one of his newspapers.

'Oh really?' said Paul. 'What's he doing there?'

'His mother lives there,' I said. I am incapable of discussing Robert : I say as little as possible about him. Next to a new book he is the most private thing in my life. 'He's visiting his mother.'

Christine said, 'I thought she was English.'

'She is, but she lives in New York.' I made a great effort and added, 'And his father lives in California,' hoping this would make an end of it. But it didn't.

'Cosy,' said Paul, watching me.

'They're divorced,' I said sharply. This did throw them. They said oh, and looked embarrassed, like people brought face to face with the unmentionable, such as death. The reaction made me wonder suddenly what state their marriage was in : people may well have a subconscious fear that misfortune is contagious. This would explain, for example, the social ostracism that widows complain of.

Christine said hesitantly, 'I read Robert's book.'

'Oh,' I said. 'You're in a minority.'

'Oh dear,' she said. 'Didn't it do very well? I got the

library to order it after you told me you were going out with him.'

'That was nice of you,' I said. 'That's one copy sold anyway.' But I nearly smiled as I spoke, not at Robert's failure, which in fact distresses me considerably, but at the phrase 'going out', which seems to me the very last thing I do with Robert. Going to bed, and fighting, and talking on the telephone, yes, but hardly going out. The phrase has a quaint charm, suggesting the pictures and dinners and walks in the park, all leading in due time to altar rails and domesticity. Going out with Robert would be like buying a tiger from a pet-shop.

'What was it called?' Paul asked. 'I think I read it.'

'*Vagrant.*' I spoke reluctantly. It is unfortunate, to say the least, to be intimately involved with someone whose work you cannot admire.

'Oh yes. I did read it. Robert ... Vyke – is that right?'

'That's right.'

'Hm.' There was a long pause, which I expected. 'Well, I can't say I enjoyed it, I'm afraid.'

'That's all right,' I said briskly. 'Nobody did, as far as I know.'

Christine said, 'Oh, darling, don't be so rude about Alexa's friends. It was ... very clever, I thought. I ... didn't really understand it but I think it was clever.'

I had known she would say something like this. It happens so often, God knows I get enough practice in reacting to it, but I still cannot decide if I find it funny or heartbreaking, which I suppose must prove it is both.

'Do you?' I said. 'That's very charitable of you. I don't. And I wish I did. It's not for want of trying.'

Paul was frowning, working his memory. 'It was about some chap drifting around the States, wasn't it?'

'Yes.' How deeply depressing the whole subject was. Robert is the sort of writer who reminds you of Mailer and Kerouac and Rechy without displaying a tenth of their talent. And yet he does have talent. Some of our bitterest arguments concern the misuse of talent, his and mine. He insists that I am obsessed with trivia; I insist that he is weighed down by significance. Or rather by the desire to be

24

significant. (The word meaningful, a loathsome American-ism, crops up a lot.) For he is not significant, and his continual effort to be so ruins his style and obscures his other virtues. It makes me angry because Robert, who started out as a reporter on *The Village Voice*, is not a novelist and should surely be old enough by now to recognize the fact. The short stories he used to write for *The New Yorker* were cynical and amusing and sad, and so crisp and elliptical: they said infinitely more than he seems to think. And yet he despises them: he cannot see that the trivial, done well, is significant, and the significant, done badly, is trivial. And worse than trivial. Turgid. Obscure. Boring (the ultimate crime). Sometimes, late at night after he has left me, I re-read the short stories, all written, with a fluency he now regards with contempt, during six golden months, and I look again at the novel, product of two grinding years, and I weep for Robert. 'It didn't even cover the advance,' I said inadequately, 'and God knows that was small enough.'

But Christine stuck to her guns, whether out of charity to Robert or a conviction that I could not really believe my lover so deservedly unsuccessful, who knows? 'That's not the only criterion, though, is it, Alexa? I mean, I know you've made money and you've deserved it, too, but lots of people write marvellous books that just don't make money, don't they?'

I sighed. 'Yes, they do. But Robert isn't one of them.' I wanted to mention the short stories; it was only fair. But I have a block about this; I feel naked if I tell people about them. It is like describing in detail how good Robert is in bed. 'He's simply not a novelist. All the space goes to his head. He doesn't know what to do with it.' I tried to explain. 'It's Parkinson's Law, I think: he expands to fill the available space. He slows down the action and he puts in too much detail – no, I mean the wrong kind of detail – and he says things obscurely twice instead of clearly once. And – oh well, *Vagrant* just shouldn't have been published, that's all; it just got in on the tail end of a wave of beatnik mania.'

Paul looked across at Christine. 'She's a tough critic, isn't she?' he said, in a ghastly, chummy-husband voice. 'I'm glad I'm not her boyfriend.'

I was upset by talking of Robert and thinking of Robert and lost my grip on the edge of control. 'Oh, I see,' I said. 'You think I'm just being catty because we're both writers. It's okay for you not to like the book and say so, but I must pretend it's good because I—' I hesitated : the word love seems to me too private for general use, I would sooner take my clothes off in public. Much sooner. 'Because I sleep with the author,' I finished in a burst of anger. Vulnerability always makes me angry.

Paul turned from Christine to me and I got, as I deserved, a hard, blue look. 'I'm sorry,' he said mildly, in direct contrast to his expression.

I expected Christine to be put out by my rudeness, as Paul obviously was; I sat waiting for my punishment and knowing that it would be just. Instead she amazed me by a sudden flow of maternalism as strong as a waft of hot air. She got up and came across to me and squeezed my shoulder. 'Poor love,' she said. 'You miss him. I shouldn't have asked about him.'

I was impressed. It is hard enough to show affection for anyone in the presence of a third party : doubly hard to embrace a girl friend in front of a husband. Probably the only threesomes that really work in terms of affection are those made up of parents and child. I remembered then that it was Christine's ability to break through to people that first attracted me to her. She has a marvellous warmth that overrides convention. So I smiled at her and swallowed and said, 'Bless you. I'm a bloody rude bitch, let's face it,' and we all laughed and the atmosphere, thank God, lightened somewhat. 'I know,' I went on, wound up and determined to atone, if only by putting as much distance, in words and action, between me and my lapse as possible. 'Let me go upstairs and get my bottle and we'll all get drunk. I've brought you some whisky. You do like whisky, don't you?'

Yes, they said, they liked whisky, but I shouldn't have, there was no need, and Paul had to go to the off-licence anyway.

'Well, he can go,' I said, getting up. I was suddenly very gay : an early lunch and too much sherry had worked on me

26

without my knowledge. 'I'm not stopping him. He can get whatever he likes and we'll make it a party.'

'God,' Christine said. 'Just like old times. I better start cooking while I can still stand up.' And she disappeared into the kitchen and Paul to the off-licence and I to the bedroom where I took rather a long time finding the whisky and counting to a hundred very slowly to calm myself. And it was surprising after that, it was almost a miracle, that we could disperse and come together again and have the kind of evening we had planned. But we did. Paul returned with beer and wine and more sherry and Christine produced some excellent chops and we all talked very loudly and amiably about people we all knew from our student days and what had happened to them, and about the eccentricities of various boys and masters at Paul's school, and about the funny side of parenthood which outweighed all the snags. This took us up to midnight, at which point Paul and Christine said that if we did not go to bed we would regret it in the morning, as the children were always awake by six. I promptly reached for more whisky in self-defence at such a barbarous prospect and we all went on talking, as we were bound to do, for another hour, but more loosely, winding down, and I watched them and wondered about them, enjoying the evening and yet feeling cheated because if I had been alone with either of them I would have got to know them, I would have made contact. And at one we went to bed.

# 6

CONTACT is all, I reflected, stumbling drunkenly around my room. Ideally I should spend my life on a non-corridor train. Alone in a compartment with one person who could be exchanged for another at the next station. And so on, for ever. Meanwhile, it would help if I could find my nightdress. If I had the sense of a flea (why flea?) I would unpack at once on arrival, knowing as I surely must that I shall be drunk by bedtime. Drunk. Alcoholic. I shall end up an alcoholic. What state is my liver in already? How Jewish that sounds – well, pop-Jewish, anyway. Robert's father is Jewish. Oh, the hell with Robert. I am going to have a hangover, oh yes I am, as sure as – ah, got it. One night-dress, drunken novelist for the wearing of. Splendid. Put it on. God, this room's cold. It's all very well but a two-bar electric fire just isn't the same as central heating and an electric blanket – oh, a hot water-bottle. Well, yes, that helps. Every little helps. But the fact remains these cottages are bloody cold. All very picturesque and lovely for American tourists en passant, but hardly meant to be lived in through the rigours of an English spring.

God, I'm drunk. Firewater. No wonder those Indians ... No. That's three times I've crossed the Atlantic already. Christ, it's quiet. If I were sober I'd probably lie awake all night. No traffic, nothing. No doors slamming, no cars passing, no people shouting good night. How do they stand it? And in the morning there'll be birds. I bet there will. I just know there'll be bloody birds singing their fat heads off, doing all that disgusting cheeping on the window-sill speci-ally to wake me up. Or if not birds, kids. Kids for sure. They told me they wake up at six. They warned me. Six. It doesn't exist. It can't. It's not an hour. It's an instrument of torture. Proves kids aren't human, waking up at six. Bet Peter and I never did. Don't remember. Couldn't have, not with such nocturnal parents. My mother told me not to come. 'Darling, you'll go out of your mind. It's *Essex*, isn't it?' Like Outer Mongolia. She was right. Don't suppose my mother ever changed a nappy or washed a sock in her life. Doesn't make her a worse mother than Christine. Better in fact. No, that's not fair. She was lucky having Eileen to do it all. If Christine had somebody she could open up the piano again. A nice simple-minded Irish girl to drool over the kids. What every modern mother needs. Not an automatic washing-machine, not a waste disposal unit, just an Eileen. God, my feet are cold. This bottle's luke-warm. Still, what can you expect? Must have been in all evening. Thank God for long hair. At least my neck's warm. Christine used to have long hair. Now it's all cut off, no, hacked, tucked away behind her ears, all ratty. Poor love, and you were going to have such a glamorous life. Concert tours and flowers and applause and black velvet dresses and all that hair sweeping down. When we're famous, we said. When we're famous ...

## 7

MORNING was terrible, every bit as terrible as I expected. Christine brought tea, saying apologetically, 'I knew you'd be awake. Who could sleep with all that racket going on?' It was eight o'clock and for two hours I had lain in bed trying to persuade myself that I was either still asleep or that I could sleep again, if I put my mind to it, while the baby screamed and the two-year-old thumped up and downstairs. I had to beg for Alka-Seltzer before I could get up, and outside the birds mocked me as I had known they would.

It took me half-an-hour to put on my face, my hands shook so much. Make-up as usual was a comfort : watching it slide on, gradually obscuring the pale, yellow, blotchy, dark-ringed mess of my hungover skin, I blessed modern science and all those dedicated chemists turning their degrees to the disguise of women instead of the salvation of the human race. It was all the same thing really, all one, whether they saved me from cancer or ugliness.

Christine cheered me. 'You look lovely', she said, when I finally appeared in the kitchen. 'Sort of tawny all over.' I was wearing a golden-brown jersey and pants that more or less matched my hair.

'I don't feel lovely.' I sank into a chair and groaned. 'God, you mustn't let me do that again.'

'Do what?' She smiled serenely, still in her housecoat, her face shiny and bare; she went on spooning something revolting into the baby while the two-year-old played round her feet with a truck and some bricks.

'Keep us all up so late. Drink so much. Oh God.' I yawned. 'It's the story of my life. The expense of spirit in a waste of booze.'

'We were all to blame.' The baby spluttered and the stuff on the spoon slurped past its mouth onto the bib, joining other, older stains. Christine wiped its mouth and reloaded the spoon. 'It was worth it, anyway.'

'It doesn't feel worth it now.' I had to remember not to turn my head too rapidly in any direction.

'Poor you, do you feel awful? Maybe you had a bit more than we did.'

'I'm sure I did. I always do. More than anyone. It's appalling, you know, Christine; it would be all right if I were a man, but as I'm not it's appalling.'

'Why?' She went on smiling at the baby and scraping the spoon round its mouth to catch all the goo that drooled out. It didn't seem to swallow very much; no wonder it took so long.

'Well, drunken men are somehow socially okay, aren't they? But drunken women just aren't. They're slobs. Lushes. It's just not glamorous. I'll ruin my image, and my looks, which is more to the point. I'll be old before my time.'

'So why do you do it?' Christine said placidly.

'Why indeed? I think I just like the taste. I don't like getting drunk and I hate being drunk and I loathe being hungover, but I never remember in time. I just go on drinking and I think it's simply because I just love the taste. If only they could make Coca-Cola taste like whisky I'd be all right.'

Christine laughed. 'I think you're all right anyway. Have some coffee; it's on the stove. I'll get breakfast as soon as I've finished with Simon.'

It shook me a little, the baby possessing a name. It was such an anonymous, greedy, helpless little animal. But it would grow up a person, like its parents. We had all started like this. I wondered what the other one was called, and knew I ought to remember. I must have had a card announcing its arrival, its name and its weight, all the usual data forced on a wide circle of acquaintance and of interest only to the immediate family.

'Has Paul gone already?' I asked, pouring black coffee.

'Oh yes, ages ago. He's on early duty this week. Oh, love—' to the two-year-old who, largely through favouring me with a baleful stare, had piled too many bricks on the back of the truck, causing the whole structure to collapse. He yelled with anger, the more so when Christine knelt down to help him. 'Let Mummy do it.' The baby, suddenly aware that the brimming spoon was no longer in contact with its lips, wailed in surprise. I knew I should do something. I contemplated what. I acknowledged defeat, my own cowardice, inadequacy, and the priority of my jersey and pants, which were new. I drank more coffee and despised myself, comfortably.

'Oh God, now he's off.' Christine was amazingly good-humoured about it all; my admiration soared. 'D'you know, I don't think they ever cry separately. It's a kind of con-spiracy : either total peace or absolute chaos. It's like having twins, except that I had a break in between. All right, love, I won't be a minute.'

'I ought to be helping you,' I said guiltily, begging for absolution. And Christine knew and she gave it to me freely.

'No, not at all. I'd cope if you weren't here; it's no different today. Just go on looking decorative and talk to me, that's all I want.'

I was deeply grateful. I looked at her and felt a vast surge of love. People are almost invariably indulgent towards me, and it must be bad for my character, like fattening cakes for the figure, and equally delicious. 'You need an au pair girl,' I said, as if by suggesting a solution, however im-practical, I could abdicate from responsibility.

'Oh yes,' said Christine. 'But who'd want to live here? Oh, it's all right for me, but girls from abroad, well, they all want to be in London, don't they?'

'I suppose so,' I said reluctantly; then, struck by her previous remark : 'But is it all right for you?'

'What?'

'Living here.'

She shrugged. 'Oh, I don't mind it really. If I can't be in London it doesn't really matter where I am. And I don't have a choice so I may as well make the best of it.'

I was upset. I hate people having to put up with anything and the braver they are the angrier I feel. I want the best for everyone, all the time, especially my friends. Provided, of course, that no sacrifice is required from me.

It is depressing to know oneself so well.

'Why?' I said. 'Why don't you have a choice? Paul could teach anywhere.'

Christine smiled. I was becoming used to the smile: it was a special one, the same one I had seen several times on the previous day, and it said specific things such as: You don't understand yet but I will explain and it's really not as bad as you think because I have accepted it.

'Yes,' she said, 'in theory he could. But there are one or two snags. I thought I explained in a letter.'

'No,' I said. 'You didn't. Or I'd remember.'

'I expect I was too cross at first to tell anyone,' she said. 'And later it wasn't important enough to write about. Well, it's two things really. One, this cottage. It was going cheap but because it was old and needed modernizing we couldn't get a big enough mortgage on Paul's salary, and we hadn't got a deposit anyway. So Paul's mother lent us the money. You know she's a widow?' I nodded. 'Well, that took all her capital. So we are paying her back at the same rate of interest as a building society because she'd have invested the money if she hadn't lent it to us. It was very kind of her,' she added, so mechanically that I was sure this was something she forced herself to say every time she told the story.

'Very,' I agreed.

'Oh, she wanted to lend it without interest,' Christine said quickly, almost defensively, 'but Paul — we felt it wouldn't be fair. In fact we refused to take it unless she let us pay interest. The only thing is we have to repay her in ten years because she's — well, she's fifty-five. So although it's cheap and in ten years we'll be free of debt—' a flash of triumph – 'at the moment it works out expensive.'

'Yes,' I said. 'I can imagine. It would.' And I thought of my flat and the ten pounds a week that I pay for it out of the money my father left me, sensible man, as a regular payment for life, not a lump sum I could blow. And it seemed to me for a moment that the money I send to Oxfam to buy myself an easy conscience would be better directed at Christine. And how impossible that would be.

'And the other thing?' I asked. 'You said there were *two* things.'

She sighed, rather heavily. 'Yes, there are. Oh, it's nothing much.' But she did not look as if it were nothing much. 'Well, the school Paul's at, it's his old school.'

This sounded almost incestuous to me. 'I didn't know. Why did he want to go back there?'

Christine frowned. 'Oh, I suppose it was partly his mother again, and the cottage, you know, and she likes to see a lot of the children but – I don't know, I think he might have gone back there anyway, quite apart from her, because of Jenkins.'

I said, 'Jenkins?'

'The Senior English Master. He taught Paul and Paul sort of reveres him. He reckons Jenkins got him into Oxford. Oh, it's absurd,' she added with touching loyalty, 'because Paul's obvious Oxford material, he'd have got in anyway, but he's got this thing about Jenkins being a marvellous teacher and how much he can learn from him. And at the same time ... well, he's more or less waiting for him to die.'

'Oh,' I said. 'That's nice. How long is it likely to take, do you know?'

She laughed nervously, the way people do when the subject is serious. 'It's not as bad as that. I mean he'll be sorry when Jenkins dies, he'll be really upset. In a way I quite dread it happening. But yes, he'll get Jenkins' job, at least he's pretty sure to. Oh, they'll advertise it but he's second in the department now so it's just a formality. Oh, he'll get it,' she repeated bitterly, as if to herself. 'Jenkins is training him for it. They both know what they're doing.'

I thought it over. 'How old is Jenkins?'

Christine said disgustedly, 'Not a day over fifty-five and as fit as a fiddle.'

We looked at each other with identical expressions of impatient distaste on our faces, and burst out laughing. 'Oh God,' I said. 'Can't you trip him up or something? Can't he do the decent thing and retire?'

Christine went on laughing till she had to wipe her eyes, and I saw her hysteria as a measure of previous tension. 'He could,' she said finally, 'but he won't. Why should he?'

I wondered how far I could risk criticism. Husbands are like relatives : it is okay for their nearest and dearest to abuse them but the outsider, even the friend, who rashly joins in may well find himself lynched. 'And Paul's quite content to wait?' I said cautiously.

'Yes,' she said, making the small word impossibly drawn out, somehow managing to say it slowly. 'Yes, he is. On the whole. What with Jenkins and the school and his mother and this place. It's ... worth it to him.'

I said, testing my luck, 'Ten years, near enough,' and she looked at me with disconcerting straightness and said, 'Yes, ten years.'

'During which time he could presumably get head of department somewhere else.'

'Oh yes.' She looked away. 'Of course he could. He's a very good teacher.'

We did not mention salaries but there was a pause during which I am certain both our brains ran over the scale of allowances for heads of department.

'Yes,' I said. 'I'm sure he is. But in ten years you'll have paid for the cottage.'

Christine finished rather suddenly with the baby, jumped up and began cutting bread for toasting. 'That's right,' she said brightly. The two-year-old, pushing his truck, started to make appropriate engine noises. 'We'll be rich, won't we? When I'm thirty-six, I'll be rich.'

## 8

ALL of which, of course, set my teeth pretty sharply on edge for the evening. I was alone with Paul, locked in another of those 'entertain Alexa' sessions : it never seemed to enter his head that he could put the kids to bed while Christine talked to me, although they saw little enough of him and he could not be more exhausted from a day at school than she was from a day at home. I began to wonder if I should ever be alone with her, without either him or them. And he did not even have the merit of sleeping for the occasional hour.

We sat and drank sherry (which I felt I could easily tire of) and my mind burned with the injustice of life. When I wrote *Golden Girl with Silver Spoon* and made a lot of people angry, I wanted to show that not only are the elect, such as Christine and I, entitled to success by virtue of talent, but that life can be more various, more rich and exciting and uncertain even for average people, than they ever begin to realize. Resignation appals me, and settling for less than the best. For the best is there, to be attempted, and even failure can be glorious. And yet here was Christine, exiled and child-ridden and musicless and poor, mortgaging her life for the prospect of comfort at thirty-six. Ten whole years of routine for such a puny reward. It could not be fair : it could not be even endurable.

Paul had my books in his hands. He turned them over and over, looking at them. 'Which one shall I read?' he said. 'I suppose I ought to read one now you're here. Which one is the best?' And he smiled at me coldly, his eyes blue and hostile.

'That's easy,' I said, smiling. 'Which one of your children do you prefer?'

'I see,' he said. 'It's like that, is it?'

I watched his hands on my books and wanted to tear them away from him before he did them harm. It was like watching someone stroke a kitten when you have reason to believe that they really wish to strangle it. 'I don't know,' I said. 'If I had children or Christine had written books, maybe one of us could tell.' But this, though he could not know, was prevarication, for I have often discussed the subject with Erin.

'Don't you ever feel,' he said, 'that you are missing real life?'

I said, 'Do you? Work is real enough, isn't it? Do you

feel that your school is unreal? Are you teaching instead of living?'

'The people I deal with exist.' He went on watching me and turning the books. 'Whereas you are writing fiction. Or is it autobiography?'

I began to see where the conversation was leading; he had a certain talent for the disguised opening. He was really asking how much of myself I put in my books: was it worth his while to read them in order to know about me? So he obviously wanted to know about me.

'No, it isn't,' I said, flattered and disturbed. 'Not entirely. Not by any means. It's a mixture. I can't explain.'

'What a pity,' he said. 'It's a question that always interests the layman and this may be my only chance to ask it. I don't meet many writers.' And his expression suggested that this was indeed a blessing.

'I can tell you how Erin works,' I said, anxious to shift his focus from me. 'You've heard of her, I assume – Erin Gould.'

'Oh yes,' he said. 'I believe I have. Although I don't read much fiction.'

I positively refused to say at this point that few men do. It may be true but somehow it implies, as it always did, that fiction is inferior to fact, and anyway all the men I know, all worthwhile men, read a lot of fiction because they realize its value. 'Well, if you ever read *The Times* or *The Observer*,' I said pleasantly, 'you must have seen Erin's name. She's about the best woman writer under thirty in England.'

He raised his eyebrows. 'Bar none?'

'Yes, indeed, bar none. I don't have any illusions about myself.'

'Oh, don't you?' he said. 'You surprise me.' And went straight on to read from the blurb all about my marvellous talent, not daring to pause, presumably, after the rudest thing he had yet said to me.

'That's the blurb,' I said, when he stopped to breathe. 'You're reading the blurb.'

He looked surprised. 'What's wrong with that? You didn't write it, did you?'

'No; although that's not as rare as you'd think. But what's

36

the point of reading it? It doesn't mean anything. They have to say all that to justify publication, especially with a first novel.'

'"*The Inside World* marks the start of an exciting career dot dot dot",' he read aloud with satisfaction. '... "Alexa King is not just another young writer but a brilliant and original novelist, with, we believe, a great future before her." ...'

'Well, it could hardly be behind me,' I said crossly. I hold no particular brief for my first publishers, except gratitude for giving me a start; they made a profit.

'Doesn't it go to your head,' he asked interestedly, 'all this stuff?' And seemed to be looking at my head, as if to see visible swelling.

'Not a *blurb*,' I said. I hoped he was not so dense in class or God help his GCE pupils. 'How could a *blurb* go to anyone's head? It's just a commercial. Do you really believe all the staff of the Egg Marketing Board go to work on an egg?'

He gave me a sceptical look as if to say, 'Ah, but you take your work more seriously than that,' and of course he was right. Then he turned to the back of *Golden Girl* and began reading my *Sunday Telegraph* review of *World*, the pride of my life. I wish I could bear to take the *Sunday Telegraph* regularly; it's been so kind to me. 'Well, that then,' he said when he had finished it. 'How about that?'

'That was lovely, of course,' I said primly. For he wasn't to know, and I would never tell him, what really went to my head: Robert telephoning me, the morning after we had first been to bed together and saying not When can I see you again? or Did I leave my lighter in your flat? or Don't tell my wife (if he'd had one), not even apologizing for calling me at eight after leaving me at three with *Golden Girl* in his pocket, but saying simply, 'Christ, baby, you're one hell of a writer, Goddam it.' The corny perfection of that sentence has remained with me, I sometimes think, more deeply embedded in my sensual memory than any orgasm, and when I am very old I shall warm myself with it.

'Well, did you agree with him?' he said.

I prised myself loose from Robert. (It is moments like that

37

which make me understand religious fervour.) I managed to laugh, my substitute for modesty. 'It works the other way,' I said. 'If they say it's rubbish you think they're mad. Or you try to, anyway. So if that means I agree with him, yes I do.' But the inaccuracy of this statement bothered me a little : a double negative is not after all quite the same as an affirmative. 'Look,' I said, wondering why I bothered (because he was Christine's husband, because he was sexy, because of my own ego?) since non-writers never really understand and writers don't have to be told. 'It's not quite that. Good reviews are lovely and you're grateful, of course, and you hope they'll help sell a few copies, but that's all really. That chap—', I remembered his name, '—isn't a writer. He's just a critic. So it doesn't count. Not as much as if another writer said it, anyway.'

'Such as Erin Gould?'

'Yes. Exactly.' In fact Erin wrote me a fantastically generous letter about my work, about the typescript of *The Sabbatical Marriage* actually, but he was not to know that either.

'And you really believe she's better than you?'

I could see he was bugged by this : assuming, I suppose, that having a fair sense of my own worth I could not have an even fairer of someone else's.

'Christ, yes,' I said impatiently, 'Haven't you read her at all?' But of course he hadn't, only heard of her, which can mean anything and probably means nothing. 'Well, you should,' I said. I am not usually so dogmatic but about Erin I am.

'All right,' he said, and I knew he wouldn't. 'Maybe I will. But I don't take your point about critics.' He hesitated and I could see the quotation come into his mind. 'It's a case of those who can, do, and those who can't, teach, is that it?'

I grinned at him. Perhaps the hostility was less than I had imagined, or already wearing thin. 'You said it. I didn't.'

He grinned back. 'Point taken. Maybe it's time for another sherry.' And he moved to pour it out. But it was in fact time for something else, and a miracle we had been spared so long. Christine and the children arrived for the bedtime routine, and I watched as usual and it all went on as before. Only this time I had other preoccupations. Aggression is so often a sexual compliment that it alerts me instantly. So I stared at Paul with increasing interest, for his probing of my work and my outlook seemed to go further than the usual stupid curiosity. And I speculated about him, and about him and Christine. Was this the premonition I had felt in the bedroom and nothing to do with the fields of Essex?

In the morning, oddly, Christine seemed to offer me an alternative explanation. Over the regular performance of the baby's breakfast she said quite casually, 'You know, I think Paul envies you, Alexa. He always wanted to write.' And I wondered in amazement how she, his wife, could with such apparent ease and lack of forethought, present me with information that he could not possibly want me to have. For writers are seldom generous towards frustrated amateurs. One meets them all the time, far too often, everwhere; they are a penance, an albatross around the neck, with their 'I could write a book, if only I had the time.' Because words are the currency of speech they imagine that anyone can write : they want the glory without the sweat. Because they have never put themselves to the test, they know nothing of our terror that one day we shall wake up and find that the gift has been taken away, the lease has expired in the night. For those who have it are of necessity humble and afraid, and do not seek to analyse it lest they destroy its very essence. It is like a strange plant that can only grow in the dark, or subterranean wall paintings that crumble and fade if exposed to the light. But the other side of humility is arrogance, and we have that too. We know, often from an early age, that we are marked out, as by leprosy or second sight : we are not like the rest. And they, by saying they could be like us, are presenting a threat, are expressing our deepest fear : that we could be like them. They remind us of the narrow path we tread.

# 9

AND then the weather improved. In a place like Essex such a detail was vital. A little pale sunlight started to hang over the fields, so I did not shudder quite so violently when I looked at them. But the days formed a pattern and all my old terror of routine returned. One's own routine, being geared to work, is a different matter, and being one's own it can be instantly broken in favour of people, or love, or sleep. But another person's routine is a strait-jacket and I felt myself already constricted; I began to choke.

We woke early, perforce, and we breakfasted with the children. I watched Christine work: there was washing and ironing and cleaning, there were meals to prepare. I looked at the fabric of the house in amazement and horror: so much activity devoted to the preservation of an inanimate object. Christine was untidy but thorough: it almost seemed that the energy she once poured into studies and scales now flowed into extricating dust from corners and polishing wood. Or perhaps she was trying to demonstrate a sudden recovery.

'I really do feel better, you know,' she said bravely at times. 'Ever since you came, I think. It's marvellous to have someone to talk to.' And indeed I didn't need to be told how oppressive silence could be. Along with two fractious children for eight or nine hours a day, she had remained remarkably sane. But silence hung over the place like a cloud: despite the interior volume of screams and tears and laughter, I was never unaware that outside the silence lay menacingly over everything.

We lunched: a long, messy process. My figure improved visibly as my appetite declined (watching children eat would make the most avid gourmet embark on a diet). We cleared up (another long, messy process) and braced ourselves for a walk. The cottage being miles from anywhere, of course, even shopping became a major expedition, and the children, moreover, needed fresh air and exercise; they were too young to amuse themselves for long in the garden, which in any case was only a soggy mass of long grass with a dangerous-looking stream at the end of it.

So we walked eventually; for it took, I discovered, an unconscionable time to prepare children for the open air. With the baby in the pram and the two-year-old on reins, except for occasional rests on the end of the pram, we strolled very slowly down muddy lanes. There were buses, of course, to Malden and Chelmsford, but they had always just gone or were about to go in half-an-hour's time, and besides, you could not take a pram on a bus. So we walked to the village, which was geographically nearer, but which seemed in terms of exertion, a positively lunar distance. I reminded myself that in London I walked miles every day, through Kensington, Chelsea, Knightsbridge, as an antidote to hours of numb sitting at the implacable typewriter, and worked myself up into sensual ecstasy at the panorama of exquisite Georgian terraces, the squares full of cherry and apple blossom, the disciplined grass. Here, every step was an effort. My feet dragged on mud and yearned for hard pavements. The hedge stretched endlessly past. And we stopped for small, childish discoveries, such as leaves and twigs.

The village, when we finally reached it, consisted of half a dozen small shops, catering only for the most vital of needs. Apart from hermits like Christine, its customers came from the new housing-development near by, the one I could see from my window. They all looked curiously related to one another, all pretty and mousy and just under thirty, with headscarves and tweed coats and practical shoes. But they were richer than Christine, their husbands being commercial not academic, and their children disgorged themselves from shooting brakes and mini-travellers. And the shopkeepers knew them all, even Christine. It was 'Good afternoon, Mrs Davies,' all the time, and 'How are you today?' and superficial gush over the kids who ran riot around the shelves. At home if a shopkeeper knew my name I should know it was time to move on.

'Have you made any friends here?' I asked Christine, though doubting she could have done and even hoping she hadn't, not cruelly or selfishly, but because I could not bear to think of her reduced to such a milieu.

She shook her head. 'Oh, I did try, sort of. I went to a few coffee mornings and things. But it didn't work. They're nice enough, but we didn't have anything in common once we'd exhausted Daz and nappy rash.' She bit her lip and giggled with a kind of guilty malice which made me want to hug her, she seemed suddenly so young again. 'Oh, I am a bitch, it's not really as bad as that. But it all comes out, about what you used to do, and you feel a bit of a freak. I mean *music*—'. She spread out her hands with a lovely involuntary movement. 'Well, it seems so odd when they all used to be secretaries and nurses. You can see them all thinking, "Oh, she must be arty and peculiar." '

'Well, she is,' I said lovingly. 'Aren't you?'

Christine made an ambiguous sound. 'Anyway, there you are. Paul said I ought to go to some of the discussion groups – you know, they have meetings to discuss, well, controversial topics, I suppose.' (We both giggled briefly, our eyes meeting with swiftly furtive contempt.) 'But I never went. I just couldn't face it somehow, I thought about college and discussions just happening, you know, late at night on someone's bed with people all over the floor, and coffee and fagends and I just couldn't bear it. I mean if it wasn't a debate I just don't see how it could ever get started. And we'd all have to rush home to our kids, that's for sure, as soon as it ever got interesting.'

We collected the shopping and piled it on the shelf under the pram. We brought conciliatory sweets for the two-year-old who was flagging from fresh air and exercise. We turned the pram homewards and walked.

'D'you know,' Christine said, 'what I really long for sometimes, of all squalid things? A bedsit. Not home, or a house, or your lovely flat even, but a squalid bedsit somewhere, Earls Court, I think probably, right in the middle of everything. And not a posh one at all, something cheap and nasty where I have to fetch water from the bathroom to cook and there's always someone in the bath when you want to wash a lettuce. And you meet people on the stairs all the time because the phone's on the landing, so there's always a queue for it, and when your heart gets broken everyone else can hear. And you cry in your room for hours, but you know you'll get over it, and the windows are open because it's summer and you hear other people's radios. Or it's winter and you have to borrow a shilling for the gas and you see inside someone else's room and it's even messier than yours. All extreme, you see,' she said, and I paled at the bright, angry tears in her eyes. 'And that's what I want again. Extremity. Or is it just youth?'

## 10

PAUL's mother came on Sunday. I was pleasantly surprised; in my usual prejudiced way I had been expecting an ogre. But she was pale and polite, very much the impoverished gentlewoman, and somehow also quite brisk and busy, full of offers of help which Christine tried hard to be too efficient to need. She called her 'my dear' all the time. ('Can I do that for you, my dear?') And Christine seemed to go out of her way to call her nothing, looking directly at her to speak, except twice when she had to call out from another room, and I listened to the strained sound of 'Mother', and wondered if I would ever be able to say that to a strange woman.

Mrs Davies sat opposite me and mostly confined her help, at Christine's insistence, to playing with the children. They clearly adored her and she was adept at managing both of them, cuddling the baby on her lap while the two-year-old played at her feet. She seemed to be able to translate his conversation, incomprehensible to me, almost as well as his parents, and it was obvious that Granny's weekly visit was nothing less than a treat. I wondered if Christine resented this. Mrs Davies, like Paul, came in for play sessions, when the work had been done, or was still being done,

43

by Christine. They could both afford to be sunny and dedicated.

'So you're Alexa,' Mrs Davies found time to say. 'I've heard so much about you. Christine lent me your books to read.'

'Oh yes,' I said, for what else can one ever say?

She looked at me sharply with Paul's blue eyes, even more startling in a face framed with grey not brown hair. 'I found them most interesting. Rather ... modern, but very well written. Christine tells me that one of them has been bought for a film. That must be very exciting for you.'

I felt Paul watching me. 'Yes, it was,' I said, 'at first, but it doesn't look now as if they are going to make it. They're just sitting on it.'

She frowned. 'Oh dear, how very disappointing. I am sorry. Still, perhaps they will make it later on.'

'There's an option on the other one, too,' said Christine rather loudly, coming in with plates. I began to feel slightly uncomfortable and wished she would not promote me quite so hard; she might as well be my agent.

'Really,' said Mrs Davies, with every appearance of interest. 'What exactly does that mean? You must forgive my ignorance.' And she kissed the baby on the top of its nearly bald head by way of punctuation.

I explained what it meant and she listened attentively. 'I see,' she said, when I stopped. 'Well, that's all very interesting, isn't it, Paul? You have done well, my dear.'

'Yes,' said Paul, with a broad and, I felt, malicious smile. 'She's a clever girl, isn't she, mother? No wonder Chris is so proud of her.'

I considered various fatuous phrases about luck and film people not knowing what to do with their money, but discarded them. Let them think what they liked and enjoy it.

We had nursery tea, and it took me back years. Piles of thickly-buttered bread, brown and white, currant loaf, chocolate cake, swiss roll, plates of biscuits. All eaten in strict order of virtue. Christine said very little, being pre-occupied with feeding one child and supervising the table manners of the other, but when she spoke to her mother-in-law did so in tones of guarded politeness and limited

44

warmth. Tea, and the formal gathering around the table, seemed to provide Mrs Davies with a chance to seek Paul's advice on her problems, as the only surviving man of the house.

'Paul, I'm afraid that new gardener has left,' she said hesitantly. 'I gave him a month's trial, as you know, but he only lasted a fortnight. He was very surly and we had words about bedding out some plants, such a trivial little disagreement I didn't think any more about, but the next day he gave in his notice. Now aren't people extraordinary?'

Paul sprang dutifully to the main point. 'Don't worry about it, mother; I'll come over one evening and do it for you.' He did not look at Christine.

Mrs Davies sighed. 'Well, that would be kind. But only if Christine can spare you. I know how busy you must be with your marking, and there are always little jobs to do round the house, aren't there?'

'Oh, Chris can spare me all right,' said Paul, in a loud, cheerful voice. 'Can't you, love?'

Christine smiled and fed the baby rather rapidly, so that it almost choked, 'Yes, of course. Do you good to get some fresh air. (There, there, love, better now?) Get all that chalk out of your lungs.'

'Well, you know I'd do it myself,' Mrs Davies said. 'I'd like to; I only wish I could. But I'm afraid all that sort of thing's quite out of the question now, with my back.' She turned to me, smiling regretfully. 'It's such a bore, you know, when you're not as young as you were, and you can't do these things. I used to love gardening but now I just can't manage the stooping. It makes me so cross because I do hate asking favours, even from Paul.' And she flashed him a look of such intense maternal pride and love as I had only seen on Christine's face when she was bathing the children or putting them to bed.

'Don't be silly, mother,' said Paul. 'You know I enjoy doing it. How about tomorrow evening?'

My heart jumped at the prospect of an evening alone with Christine. Mrs Davies relaxed. 'Oh, if you could,' she said, 'that would be marvellous. That would really be a weight off my mind. And—', she hesitated, '— there's just one more thing. I'm so sorry to have to ask you, but if you could take a look at the washer on that tap.'

'Oh yes,' said Paul. 'Has it gone again?'

'I'm afraid it must have done. Something's gone wrong anyway.' Again she turned to me with an apologetic smile. 'I'm afraid I'm quite useless with mechanical things. Are you any good?'

'I don't know,' I said honestly. 'I've never noticed.'

'Oh well,' she said. 'I thought maybe you modern young women could do all these things, like changing fuses and things. Anyway . . .' And she turned back to Paul.

'Yes,' he said instantly. 'I'll do the tap tomorrow night too. And any other odds and ends you want doing. Glad to.'

After this, the conversation drifted and died, Mrs Davies having achieved her objective. We finished tea and Christine began clearing the table. Mrs Davies leaned back and stretched in her chair. 'That was lovely,' she said. 'You do everything so well, Christine.' She smiled at me, continuing the compliment obliquely. 'I really look forward to Sundays, you know. It's such a treat for me to come here.'

'Stay to supper, won't you?' Christine said at once, and I felt that this must be an offer that had to be made every week.

'Oh no, dear, thank you all the same. I really mustn't impose on you any longer.' Perhaps the answer, too, was routine.

'Nonsense,' said Paul briskly. 'You know we'd love to have you. We don't see enough of you.'

'Oh, you're very sweet.' She closed her eyes briefly, with a look of physical satisfaction, like somebody basking in the sun. 'But I do have things to do at home; I must get back. And Christine will have to put these two little angels to bed quite soon, won't she? Yes—', beaming at the children, 'Mummy's going to put you to bed soon, isn't she? Granny must go home now.'

The baby looked understandably blank at this piece of information but the two-year-old raised a satisfactory howl of protest. Christine flung out of the room with a pile of dirty plates and Paul retired from the table, and lit a cigarette. 'Well,' said Mrs Davies, smiling, 'maybe not just yet.

Are you coming for a walk in the garden with Granny first? Shall Granny take you in the garden then?'

The suggestion seemed popular. Mrs Davies raised her voice and called out, 'Is that all right, Christine? May I take Michael in the garden for a little walk?'

I listened to the strain in Christine's voice and wondered if it was obvious only to me. 'Yes, of course. That would be lovely.'

I joined Christine in the kitchen and we watched through the window as Mrs Davies and Paul walked down the path, the toddler holding their hands and stumbling between them. Christine was washing up with unusual violence. 'There you are,' she said, slamming plates into the plate-rack. 'She's sweet, isn't she? You can't possibly hate her, can you?'

## II

I PINNED my hopes to Monday evening. So far I had not been completely alone with Christine for any serviceable length of time, and much as I treasured the occasional gleams of truth, such as the bedsit outburst, I had not gathered nearly enough material to account for the letter that had summoned me. Christine clearly loved her children : the love shone out of her face while she performed the most menial tasks for them, it was there in the gentleness of her hands. And she had her reward in hugs, smiles, and jokes. But regarding the rest of her life she had given me only inessentials : the job and the cottage could not, after three or four years, make her suddenly hysterical. The piano was closed; she had not mentioned music. Of her life with Paul I knew nothing of importance yet.

I wondered if she regretted the letter. Perhaps she was engaged in retreating from me after spilling too much of herself on paper, for the letter, though vague, had been violent. Normally I would not have been impatient : these things should emerge as part of the natural order, without haste. But I was tired of being presented to people, the glamorous, clever Bohemian friend, imported to provide a little gentle friction with Paul and his mother and to be paraded round the shops. I had spent a week in the place already, doing far too little of my own work (for which there was a deadline), listening to the silence and the children and the birds, and making very little progress with Christine. But I felt the texture of her life all around me, the weave of boredom and happiness, frustration and fulfilment. I could see what it was like to be Christine in everyday terms. But I did not know how she felt : she would have to tell me.

I laid my plans carefully. Since a whole evening was rare, we could not afford to waste it. I had come so that Christine could talk to me and she had not done so : who could tell when the next opportunity might occur? So I bought several bottles of wine, which I thought would be better for us than Scotch; I even offered to cook and had the offer accepted, as I had known it would be, since Christine, like most of my friends, understands that I only make genuine offers, of the sort that I wish to carry out. So I bought food, too, insofar as the shops allowed me to, and felt a rising excitement. Robert is quite right, though he says it bitterly, that I am as aroused by the prospect of an evening with a girlfriend as I am by the prospect of sex with him. I reply that sex and talk are great and equal pleasures and whichever you are enjoying at the time seems the greater; or, alternatively, whichever you have been more deprived of seems the more desirable. But these two remain the mainsprings of my life (as indeed of his) because from them, it seems to me, arises work. And the greatest of these is work.

The children seemed to sense that the evening was special : like animals they have a nose for these things. Paul's mother had invited him to supper so he departed early amidst cries of Daddy. Revenge for their disappointment at a curtailed playtime was inevitably wreaked on Christine and me. They were extraordinarily difficult to get to bed (the baby even seemed to catch from his brother the message that tonight resistance must be offered) and, once there, the mobile one at least was hard to keep there. I left Christine to it and clung to the kitchen : I adore cooking because I do it so seldom. The pleasure has never been given the chance to pall by familiarity. Once or twice a week at the most, for my friends, and then I go to infinite trouble. The rest of the time I starve or eat out or sponge on my mother.

So I peeled mushrooms and prepared tomatoes, crushed garlic and buttered steak, tore up salad and smothered it in dressing, scraped new potatoes, scooped out melon and skewered corn cobs, and generally revelled in the image of myself as culinary genius and domestic drudge. I am very susceptible to publicity – indeed I consider it one of the new art forms of our age – and I once read an article (no doubt entirely phony) about Marlene Dietrich's activities in the kitchen, which impressed me exceedingly. It is the element of incongruity which is so important : the cook must be glamorous and talented or the image is ruined. In the same way, when I create my warm golden fantasy of childhood, based on my own childhood, I see myself as a glamorous mother, like my mother, unmarked by tedium, always with time to be responsive and receptive, always scented and smiling : I visualize (indeed, remember) the sort of freedom and excess that only money can buy. Mrs Davies thought my work was modern : in reality I am nothing less than a romantic.

When Christine finally reappeared she was flushed and dishevelled, splashed with bath water; even her hair was damp. She sat on a stool at her own kitchen table like a visitor and said gratefully, 'God, that looks marvellous. You're going mad.'

'I'm indulging myself,' I said. 'You're not to do a thing. Just sit and be waited on.'

She looked around. 'Lovely. But it does feel odd. I'm not used to it.' She stretched luxuriously. 'Alexa, how's Lucas? I've been meaning to ask you and I just caught sight of myself in the mirror upstairs and remembered her, by contrast, naturally.'

I laughed. 'Oh, come off it.' But the truth of the observation pained me. 'She's fine. She's in New York at the moment actually, modelling. I've told her she must look up Robert.' I realized that this meant they would sleep together but since they probably would anyway it seemed more realistic and efficient to suggest it.

'God, she was lovely,' Christine said enviously. Lucas is a typical model, with a classic blonde leggy beauty that is almost corny in its appropriateness : conformity to an image taken to excess. 'Is she still as lovely? I suppose she is.'

'Yes, she is. She's just had another abortion, actually, but she's got over it very well.' I was taking a risk but it seemed worth trying to plunge Christine back even forcibly into the messy world of drama which we had once all inhabited.

Christine looked troubled : conflict between the mother and the friend showed clearly on her face. I waited interestedly for resolution.

'Has she?' she said finally. 'Oh dear. How ironic. D'you know, it was only recently that I realized that's something I could never do. Remember how casually we all used to talk about it. I never really thought, not seriously, until I lost the baby. But now I know I could never do it.'

'Well, Lucas wasn't keen,' I said, 'but she didn't feel she had much choice.'

'Oh no, no,' Christine said hastily. 'I'm not blaming her. I expect she was right.' She poured herself a glass of wine and drank it like water. 'I just had no idea that having a miscarriage could upset me so much.'

I was interested in this and had wanted to ask about it but knew I must proceed carefully. Christine, for all her warmth, was inclined at times to retreat if cornered too abruptly. 'It must be so different though,' I said. 'All the difference in the world between feeling trapped and losing something you wanted.'

'But I didn't,' Christine said violently, amazing me, and at once contradicted herself. 'Well, I did, but I knew I was wrong. I knew I wasn't entitled to do it and Paul didn't want it. I was indulging myself and I felt guilty all the time and I was punished for it, you see.'

I was fascinated by this and hardly knew which point to grab first. 'Paul didn't want it,' I repeated. 'But I thought he was just as upset as you were when you lost it.'

'Yes, he was,' she said. 'but he was relieved as well. Oh, I don't know—', she waved her hands distractedly. 'He was upset because I was ill, I think. He doesn't like me to be ill, it upsets him, he expects me to be tough and fit all the time and I generally am. But I know he was relieved as well because he thought it was too soon and we couldn't afford it, I mean physically or financially, we couldn't afford it at all in any way really.'

'But you wanted it,' I said gently.

She drank some more wine and stared at her feet. 'Yes. I did. Desperately.' Her voice suddenly shook and a tear splashed onto her skirt : she stared at it without comprehension. 'Alexa, it frightens me at times. D'you know, I read all about myself in *The Observer* one Sunday. It was just after I knew I was pregnant and I read this article about a woman who just went on having children. She had three and she was pregnant again and delighted but all her relatives and friends were appalled and her husband was furious. She even had a part-time job that she liked and she knew she couldn't go on having children for ever, she knew she'd have to stop eventually, but she couldn't, it was like a compulsion. And I read this and it was me, Alexa. I recognized myself.' She looked at me wildly. 'It was terrifying. I mean I could see it was a sort of illness, in this woman's case, and so could she, and here was I doing exactly the same thing. And that's when I started to feel guilty. I'd repressed it before, I'd pretended it was all right, but when I read that article I just had to admit I was wrong. I'd been found out, you see.' She laughed. 'The article condemned me.'

I said, 'Did you know Paul didn't want it when you started it?'

'Oh yes. We'd agreed to wait. We talked it over and agreed it was too soon with Simon only just a year old and money and the cottage and everything. It was an awful thing to do. I had to pretend it was an accident but I don't think Paul believed me. I don't know even now and I daren't ask him; I just swear blind it was and he can't prove it wasn't, thank God.' She paused, breathing deeply, and took another gulp of wine.

'How interesting,' I said sincerely. 'How absolutely

fascinating. I think I read that article too; it does seem vaguely familiar now you mention it. But why? You must have some idea why you did it?'

Christine was gripping the edge of the table with peculiar intensity. 'Why not?' she said. 'What else can I do?'

\*            \*            \*

The food was ready. We started to eat and I watched Christine who now seemed extraordinarily wound up. She ate in rapid bursts and then paused to stare dreamily into space before gobbling some more. 'This is delicious,' she said.

But I was not to be so easily diverted. I, too, had been drinking so I took a chance. 'What do you mean?' I said. 'What else can you do? You can play the piano again, for instance. There are lots of things you can do.'

She groaned. 'Oh, don't. Not you too. That's what Paul says. Why not take up your music again?'

Yes, I thought, I could just hear him saying that. But there were ways and ways of putting it. 'Don't you want to play any more?' I said, with a dreadful certainty that I knew the answer.

'Yes, of course I bloody do,' she said fiercely. 'But not badly, and that's how I do play now. Badly. It's not just a diversion, Alexa, you can't pick it up and put it down like a toy. And I don't want to do it badly, God, I just don't. I'd rather not do it at all.'

'I know,' I said. 'I do know, love, honestly. I'm sorry.'

'Anyway,' she said. 'I don't have time to do it any more, not properly. And the children are far more important. I can't neglect the children to play the piano, can I, and anyway, what for? I mean it wouldn't lead anywhere, would it, so what's the point? There are more important things to do, anyway.'

'Like having more children?'

'Yes.' She banged her fist on the table. 'Yes, exactly. Why not?' And then, immediately: 'Oh God, I'm a dishonest cow. I know perfectly well why not. I've been told why not often enough.'

I tried another line. 'What does your doctor say?'

'Oh, him.' She laughed.

'No good?'

'Yes, fine.' It was the same tone she had used about her mother-in-law. ' "You have two splendid children, Mrs Davies, you just concentrate on them and go to the family planning clinic." '

We both drank some more wine and considered this. 'And did you?' I said.

'Oh yes.' She screwed up her mouth in distaste. 'I seem to spend my life there being poked about.'

'And?' I was sympathetic but I thought it would do her more good to talk than be soothed.

'Oh, well, they fitted me up, of course. But it hurts, Alexa. It really does. It's uncomfortable all the time.'

'Go back,' I said. 'It must be the wrong size.' But I knew what was coming.

'Oh, I did, and they checked. It's all right. It's all in my mind. They as good as told me I was imagining it all. But that doesn't make it less real, now does it? I just hate it, I hate the whole thing.' She ate some more food. 'This is lovely; you *are* a good cook.'

'It was that Cordon Bleu thing,' I said, 'before I quit.' I am half-trained for so many things : art, flowers, food (if I didn't leave they always threw me out) – everything except writing, which cannot be taught. 'Pills,' I said. 'What about pills?'

'They frighten me,' Christine said promptly.

'Oh, come on,' I said. 'You've been reading the news-papers.'

'No, really.' She looked quite serious, insisting, 'I did try them, Paul and the doctor went on at me so, but I got the most terrible side effects.'

'Well,' I said, sorry to sound authoritarian, 'you do have to persevere.'

She shook her head. 'I couldn't. It was awful. I felt ill all the time. And it wasn't just physical. I felt I was going out of my mind.'

I tried to coax her out of this, teasing : 'But you feel that anyway.' It was the letter all over again, the authentic note of despair.

'Yes, I do.' She actually laughed. She knew she was taking herself too seriously and her ability to recognize this had always been enviable and endearing. 'But not all the time. So it's better really.'

I said, 'Except that you get pregnant instead.'

'Yes.' She gave a guilty grin, a school-girl caught playing truant or cheating. 'Aren't I awful?'

'Well,' I said. 'Yes.'

She smiled tenderly to herself, as if at the children. 'Poor Paul,' she said. 'It's really not fair on him, is it?'

'I'm surprised he doesn't take action,' I said. 'It sounds as though he ought to protect himself against you.' And I had to admit the idea was amusing : marital rape with the roles reversed.

'Oh, I wouldn't stand for that,' she said quickly.

'No, all right.' I became energetic. 'I agree it's lousy. But science has progressed since then. No one has to stand for that any more.'

'Oh, I know, I know.' She played with the food on her plate, turning her fork round and round. 'I just don't see what science has got to do with me. It's no good talking sense to me, Alexa. I just can't see it. I'm hopeless. I know I am.'

And this, I reflected, was the worst part of the disease : she did not want to be cured.

'But you,' she said suddenly and fiercely. 'What about you? You go on writing books. You just want to go on and on doing the same thing, writing more and more books. You're just lucky it's not anti-social : books don't cry in the night or have to be fed; they don't take up much room. But people don't choose their obsessions. It's not my fault I'm hooked on something so inconvenient.'

I had all the time the same feeling that she was revelling in her unreason even while she condemned it with logic. But what she said was true : it was a parallel that had struck me before. My mother's lovers, Christine's children, my books, Lucas's abortions : we are all repetitive once our tastes are established. Condemnation is useless, but the reasons for repetition are absorbing.

'I know,' I said. 'You're right. But what is it really you

want? Is it the fact of another baby in the house or is it the being pregnant you want most?'

She shook her head and there was a long pause. Finally she said, 'I don't know. Oh, I've tried to think but ... Well, it must be both, mustn't it?'

'Must it?' She was cheating, surely; she was too intelligent to believe such an easy compromise. And she was too honest to do it for long; she said at once:

'No, you're right, of course. I just don't want to face it. Oh, I love them once they're here and they're real – when I'm not cursing them, that is – but I don't honestly yearn to have six or ten or twenty, or whatever it is. I mean I know there's a number beyond which I couldn't cope and it's probably – God – it's probably two, God help me, or three at the most. I was terribly run down after Simon; I got so tired it just wasn't true. I don't imagine myself surrounded by a brood or anything idyllic like that. So it must be the pregnancy thing.' And she then looked ashamed so I almost wished I had not pressed her. But it was too late now to retreat so I reminded myself that conversation was therapy, and I believed in it, and this was not a time to abandon a basic tenet of my philosophy.

I said, 'How do you feel when you're pregnant?' and her face took on a most alarming look, a sort of semi-religious glow; I don't know how else to describe it. A kind of extravagant and fervent private rapture.

She said, 'Sick,' and I burst out laughing at the incongruity. She had misled me beautifully. And yet I knew the look was real enough; I could imagine what would follow, and it did. She went on: 'I know it's funny. I feel awful physically, for at least three months but that doesn't matter at all. I get such a lift – well, I imagine it's like being on drugs. I feel important and special, all the time. I think I go around smiling almost. I feel so incredibly powerful I could do anything: you know, all the usual limits disappear. And everything round me seems brighter and stronger and – oh, is any of this making sense?'

'Yes,' I said, depressed and exalted by recognition. 'You're describing creation.'

We took our coffee into the sitting-room. Christine paced

about and I began to be worried that I had loosened her up too much. She wandered round the room in purposeless circles, occasionally touching things, books and cushions, and smiling to herself. She had the sort of messy disorientation I had seen in productions of *Hamlet*; she reminded me of Ophelia. I was frightened.

'Oh, look at all this,' she said, waving her hand at the objects in the room. 'Isn't it odd? You fall in love and it all comes down to this. Furniture and meals and ... *things*. Things all round you. They don't seem to have anything to do with it at all and yet here they are and you can't do without them. D'you ever feel like that? Sometimes – just after I lost the baby I did it a lot – I sit here and look at everything and I want to snap my fingers and make it all disappear, like a witch. That's what we need, you know, Alexa, magic powers. That's what we're missing.'

'You've got Paul,' I said, alarmed, 'and the children. That's a kind of magic, if you love them. And you do, don't you?' I desperately wanted to hear her say it. 'That's a lot more than many people have got. Just love.'

'Oh yes, I love them.' She frowned at the word. 'But it dissipates. *It dissipates.* You must know what I mean.' She banged her fist into the palm of her hand, then rubbed one against the other. 'Where is it? It goes into things. Doesn't it? There are bits of it all round us, in the toys and the furniture and the carpet. But where is the thing I felt at the beginning when Paul and I were first married, when the children were born, when ...?'

'When you were pregnant?'

'Yes.' Her eyes almost flashed with excitement. 'Oh *yes*. Most of all then. That's like being in love again. D'you know, I actually thought I might die.'

I drank my coffee; I had had enough of wine, and Christine had evidently had too much. It was useless to try to make her sit down. 'When you were in love or when you were pregnant?' I said.

'When I was pregnant. But yes – you're right – it's the same being in love. Aren't you clever? Of course, you're right. Fancy you knowing that.'

She obviously thought I was helping her. I was not so

sure. She was saying things I understood only too well, for my own life is geared as far as possible to intensity instead of routine, but they seemed incompatible with her situation. I tried to argue against myself.

'Of course I know it,' I said. 'You're talking about drama, aren't you? But you can't live on that level all the time; no one can. I mean, look at me. Robert's away now and I try not to think about him; when I write a book, even, I can't be excited about it all the time. I have to revise it and type it; there's a lot of routine as well. There has to be. It's the same for you, with Paul and the children.'

'But it's not,' she said wildly. 'Robert goes away and comes back. That's dramatic. Well, isn't it? And when you finish a book, there's the next one. You can go on renewing yourself. You can start the whole process again. You can have the whole thing again, as often as you like. Can't you?' And she punched the back of the sofa. 'But I'm not allowed to. I'm being punished for being myself. Don't you see? They won't let me get it back. I'm condemned.'

She was weeping. I got up and put my arms round her; she leaned her face against me and howled. Her mouth was open and I could feel her teeth pressed against my collar-bone and her tears soaking through my dress to my skin, first hot then gradually cold. I stroked her hair like a child; there was nothing to say.

'Love,' I said. 'Poor love.'

We stood like this for moments. Then upstairs a child cried. Christine's head jerked up, nearly striking my chin.

'That's Michael,' she said. 'He wants me. I must go.' She broke away from me and rushed to the door where she paused, briefly. 'You see? Mothers shouldn't cry. It's a luxury.' And then she was gone.

I sat down with a huge sigh. I was exhausted. I longed for my mother, which presumably is the ultimate tribute to her success as a parent: I always feel she can cope where I can't. She came pretty near to breakdown herself when Daddy died, but she is a more resilient person than Christine and besides she had an expensively brilliant psychiatrist in whom to confide. Whereas Christine has only me. I lit a cigarette and looked round the room, trying to drag help out of the air. At times like this I am overwhelmed by my inadequacy at coping with real life. My own life is chaotic and I do not try to organize it : brilliant colours and a messy pattern are all I require. This relates to my work, or perhaps it is the other way round; at any rate there is no discrepancy. I do not know how to create order from chaos, except on paper, for chaos is what I basically need. But it will surely destroy Christine. There is no room in her life for it, and I cannot change her life.

She came back, swaying a little, and said as she entered, 'God, I'm drunk. I nearly fell downstairs just now,' and I was relieved at the lighter tone.

I said, 'That's my fault, with the wine,' and added, 'How's Michael?', thinking the sound of his name might steady her.

She sat down, which was an improvement, but smiled rather oddly, which was not. 'Oh, he's fine now,' she said. 'He just wanted a cuddle and a drink, somebody there. Well, me really. He had a nightmare. That's funny, isn't it? He must have been dreaming about my life.'

I leaned forward and put a hand on her knee. 'Look, love,' I said, thinking how uncharacteristic my soothing tone sounded. 'Calm down. Don't get so upset. It's not worth it.'

She shook her head. 'No. It's only my life. Nothing to get upset about.'

I said, 'I know. Honestly I do. But you're not helping yourself. You're still upset about losing the baby and you're terribly run-down and tired. That wretched home-help shouldn't have left. You must let me do more. I've been a selfish pig. But I'm here and I *can* help. I'd like to. You must tell me what to do and I'll do it.'

Christine ignored this. She said dreamily, 'I'd like to run away. I've often planned it. Sometimes I take the children and sometimes I don't. But I always run away. I just pack and leave a note and I go. On the train. You can get lost in London, can't you?'

'Yes,' I said, 'but you don't really want to.'

'Don't I?' she said, and laughed. 'How do you know? Why shouldn't I want to run away? Okay, so I've got responsibilities. Don't tell me. What better reason is there for running away?'

'But it's not that,' I said sharply. 'You love them, you know you do. You couldn't leave them all.'

She rocked herself to and fro in the chair. 'But it's grey,' she said, 'all over. There's no colour left. Nothing happens. And I keep trying to make it. They don't want me like that. They want me all calm and loving. They want me to be a tower of strength.'

'Have you talked to Paul?' I asked. 'Have you said all this to him?'

She waved her hands; she laughed a little. 'Why d'you think I wanted you to come? How can I talk to him like this? I'd be accusing him, wouldn't I? I'd be saying he bores me. Can you imagine that? Our life together bores me; I want more than you can give me. But I can say it to you because it's not your fault. I won't make you feel guilty.'

The front door clicked : our evening was suddenly at an end. I said urgently, 'Look, love, you need a rest. Why not go to my flat for a week; I'll give you the key. Just be there, alone, and do what you want. Paul and I can cope here.' And he came at that moment into the room.

'I hear my name,' he said, in that slightly pedantic way of his, 'taken in vain, no doubt. So let's have a little light on the scene.' He clicked the switch and light flooded us uncomfortably, revealing my anxiety and Christine's ravaged face. I got up to distract him.

'I've just been saying,' I announced brightly, 'that a few days in town might do Christine good. She could stay at my flat. You and I could cope with the children, don't you think?'

'You couldn't,' Christine said promptly, her voice thick with tears. 'You need me. You couldn't manage without me.'

He went over to her and put a hand on her shoulder. 'That's right,' he said. 'You're indispensable, of course.' He turned her face towards him with one finger. 'But your health is quite important, too. You're upset, aren't you, love? What's the matter?'

I moved to the door. 'I'll go,' I said in a low voice, hoping

I could actually do so before they noticed me. But Paul said quite sharply, 'No, stay, Alexa. Please stay. You're a friend of the family, after all. I don't suppose there's anything Chris can't say in front of you. I imagine she must have been telling you her troubles all evening already.' Then he went on talking to Christine in a gentle, affectionate voice and it struck me that he was less concerned with proving to me that he was kind to Christine. Perhaps he feared she had painted him to me as a monster. I went and sat in a chair as far away as possible and looked at my nails. Then I looked at my watch. It was only half-past ten but it could have been any hour of the night.

'Listen to me, darling,' he went on, in a voice of excessive tenderness that branded me as an intruder, albeit against my will. 'Of course we can't *manage* without you. We need you, we'll miss you. But we *can* muddle through. You know you need a holiday, even the doctor said so. There's no point in waiting till the end of term when you need a rest now. If Alexa's offered you her flat why not take it, darling? Have a week there, have as long as you like. You'll come back so rested; you'll be your old self again. No one can go on for ever without a break and that's what you're trying to do. You're driving yourself too hard.'

Christine said in a muffled voice, 'You do that too. You know you do.'

Still the same gentle voice but a shade firmer now. 'I haven't had two, nearly three babies in three years. No wonder you're tired, love.'

Christine jumped up. 'But it's not tiring,' she shouted. 'It's not. It's anything but. It's—' She was suddenly weeping. 'Oh, God,' she said. 'Let me go to bed. Please let me. I can't take any more.'

We were alone, Paul and I. We listened to Christine's feet as she stumbled upstairs. 'Should you go after her?' I suggested, less from concern than from an urge not to be alone with him. But he said, 'No, she needs to be alone. She'll have a good cry and feel better and then she'll go to sleep. And that's what she needs most of all. Just a good night's sleep.'

It sounded so simple. I said nothing. Paul lit a cigarette.

'I'm afraid you unsettle her,' he said, coming to stand in front of me. 'I knew you would, that's why I didn't want her to send for you. It's not that you're unwelcome ...'

'But you don't want me here,' I said for him, lightly and brightly. I had wondered when we would both come out into the open and here we were, a little sooner than I had expected.

He smiled. He had a very attractive smile. Lots of corny old adjectives sprang to mind, such as boyish and disarming. He was that kind of person. I could see, in a way, why Christine had fallen in love with him, and although he was not really my type, insofar as I have one, I began to doubt the wisdom of suggesting a week alone with him in the house. I had a lot of work to do and could not afford tension.

'That sounds very rude,' he said, 'doesn't it? Let me try to explain. Any friend of Chris is welcome, of course. She gets out so seldom, I'm delighted for her to see people. But naturally, I'm concerned for her welfare. And I'm afraid you unsettle her. You remind her of the past and that's always dangerous. You remind her of music and ambition and money and freedom. You're dangerous, Alexa. You represent all the things she can't have.' And then he smiled in apology. 'I'm sorry,' he said. 'I'm speaking very frankly; I don't mean to be rude. But Chris has to come first. I owed you an explanation, anyway; I'm afraid I haven't been very polite to you.'

I got up. I cannot bear people standing over me in any case, and particularly not Paul. 'What do you want me to do?' I said. 'Go away? Why did you let me come in the first place?'

He gestured helplessly; rather a charming movement in contrast to the tough talk. 'What could I do? Chris was almost hysterical. You were the one person she wanted to see.'

It was my turn to pace about. I caught sight of myself in the mirror and thought how incongruous I was in the room with my dramatic eye make-up and my bright mane of hair, the image I had so carefully cultivated. It was out of place here. But Christine was my friend. I said, 'Well, okay, so

I'm here and you had to let me come. Now what do you want me to do? I can arrange a telegram from my agent if you like; that's been done in a dozen bad plays so why shouldn't we try it?'

'There you are,' he said at once, with satisfaction. 'I wonder if you really know the difference between fiction and life? You think in terms of drama, don't you, all the time. I believe you create it wherever you go.'

This was so near the truth, or at least something I had often suspected, that I was quite alarmed. 'Never mind about me,' I said. 'I thought we were both concerned about Christine. Just tell me what you think is best for her and I'll do it.' And indeed I rather hoped he would tell me to go, for I began to think I really was dangerous and the whole situation too much for me to handle. Besides, the prospect of imminent escape from Essex was alluring in the extreme. I began at once to visualize my flat and the warmth of it, my own things around me, the neighbouring cat on a visit and my mother's voice on the phone, pouring out all the details of her latest affair. London, I thought, and salvation. I could walk on its pavements again and buy clothes. There were plays I could see. And all the noise and the people would make my work more real. I had certainly done little enough here.

'No,' he said, dashing my hopes. 'It's not up to me. Now you're here Chris will have to decide. But I think we should both encourage her to have a week in your flat; that's the best we can hope for. Then perhaps when she comes back she'll be ready to let you go.'

He talked as if my time was endlessly available and I could stay for ever just because I had no employer, stop-watch in hand. I made one last, hopeless effort.

'Wouldn't it be better,' I said, 'if I went back and got the place ready – it's in a bit of a mess – and then Christine could come and we'd be there together? That might be more fun for her. Couldn't your mother help with the children?' But this was the classic forlorn hope of cliché fame and I knew it.

'Out of the question,' he said. 'My mother goes out to work. She hasn't got a private income.'

I ignored this crack. Very often I let people go beyond reasonable bounds, both in actions and words, out of sheer curiosity.

'Okay,' I said. 'Then Christine could bring the kids with her. I expect my mother could find someone to look after them.' And this, I thought, was the ultimate : greater love has no friend. For my mother would no doubt lay on help but it would be my flat they would rampage through. My mother, who adored us as children, now considers her duty done and has even been known to send Xmas cards to my brother and his wife specially printed with : Sold in Aid of the Abortion Law Reform Society and The Family Planning Association. Oh yes, a joke, but the motivation is clear enough. I would not be able to unload Christine's kids on my mother.

But Paul shook his head : the supreme sacrifice, it seemed, was not to be required of me. 'No,' he said, 'that won't do. I think Chris needs a rest from the kids more than anything.'

A door banged upstairs. 'Ah,' he said. 'She's gone to bed. She's been crying in the bathroom, I expect, but she'll sleep now.'

It depressed me that he knew the procedure of distress so well and yet could do nothing to alleviate it. Sometimes I despair of any equal relationship even existing, let alone surviving, on a fully-satisfying level. Off-hand, I can only think of my parents and they were two such extravagant personalities, perennially fascinated by each other's eccentricities. They knew each other, for it is surely only through complete knowledge that such extreme tolerance can be exchanged, and yet the house, as I remember it, virtually echoed to cries of 'How amazing, how extraordinary, how surprising.' Perhaps when people shake their heads over my parental reminiscences they mean I have already set my sights too high.

I said, 'Good,' but I must have sounded depressed for Paul said :

'I'm sorry, but that's the way it is. Believe me, I do know what's best for Chris.'

I said, 'Yes, I'm sure you do.' He sounded to me like a

jailer or at least a nurse in a mental hospital saying firmly, 'I'm afraid this patient really must be put in a strait-jacket for her own good.' No doubt I was being unfair. But friendship creates its own prejudice.

'People need to be alone,' he said, 'sometimes.'

I knew this was true, too true to need saying. 'Yes.'

'And this is one of those times.' He paused. 'You don't agree with me.'

I shrugged. 'It's nothing to do with me. I expect you're right. It doesn't matter what I think.'

'Oh, but it does,' he said. 'You are sitting in judgment on us all.'

He was following me, step by step, across the room. I backed crossly into the fireplace. 'I'm not doing anything of the sort.'

He smiled and stood on the hearthrug, boxing me in. 'You may not want to,' he said. 'I'm prepared to give you the benefit of the doubt. But that's what you're here for. You've been imported as an arbitrator. Why else do you think we both talk to you so much? We want you to justify us. You're a Daniel come to judgment, Alexa.'

I stood my ground for a further moment then made a positive effort and brushed past him, catching a disturbing whiff of shaving lotion and tobacco, the sort of thing the women's magazines warn you about. 'Don't be absurd,' I said sharply and pleasantly (this is a possible though unlikely mixture). 'I'm Christine's friend and I'm here because she got depressed and wanted to see me. That's all there is to it. You mustn't exaggerate, Paul.' It was the first time I had used his name.

He spoke as I reached the door. 'You surprise me,' he said. 'You really want to bury your head in the sand. I thought as a writer you'd be more clear-sighted.'

It was not a time to argue. Besides I had really had enough of this kind of thing. So I turned on my last-ditch, publicity smile. 'I'm going to bed now,' I said politely. 'Goodnight.'

## 12

I WROTE to my mother. It was in fact a letter but in spirit
more of an SOS. We do this to each other all the time : it's
immensely comforting. Yet when people say 'Oh, your
mother is more of an elder sister really, isn't she?' I deny it
strenuously, and not just in defence : they are quite simply
wrong. My letter crossed, as these things always do, with
one from her; it had taken her a week to appreciate the
fact of my exile. She wrote that she had finished with David
and started with Carlo and the maid was pregnant. The
letter went on for pages, nearly bursting its envelope, as my
mother's writing is huge. Her letters are always a delight
because they are diaries: she rarely completes one in less
than four days and you really feel you have been admitted
to each hour of her life. 'So now I shall never get rid of her,'
she wrote sadly. 'You know how careless she is. Well, after
you left she went on breaking more things (even the jade
your father gave me when you were born; I'm afraid I wept
over that) and she muddled all the tradesmen, God knows
how, so we got all the wrong food on the wrong days, or is
it the right days, well, you know what I mean, so we had
the most *extraordinary* dinner parties. I just had to laugh;
there was nothing else to do. But I thought, well, this really
is impossible, and I had it all planned, a nice little bonus in
lieu of notice and an absolutely delightful reference (well, I
know it's dishonest but the poor girl's so sweet and if I must
betray someone I'd rather it was a perfect stranger and
maybe they won't have any jade). And I was going to say
I was going away, on a cruise or something, for at least
three months, so I wouldn't need her any more. And I
thought even if she saw me on T.V. she'd probably think it
was pre-recorded, so that would be all right. So there I was,
yesterday, feeling so pleased with myself (you know how
lovely it is when you find a solution that hurts nobody) and

I came into the kitchen to tell her and there she was, beating meringue and weeping. But such *big* tears – honestly, darling, they were just dripping into the bowl, I had to take it away from her. And when I finally got her to calm down, she just said, "Madam, I'm pregnant."

'So what could I do? I couldn't say anything I'd planned. I had to make her sit down and I poured brandy down her throat and then, of course, the whole story came out. He's Maltese and a Catholic and he's married, of course, and he's going back to Malta so I doubt if she'll even get whatever pittance the law allows because he won't be here to be summonsed, or whatever it is. I must admit I was surprised – well, amazed – because she's such an ugly girl, isn't she, but there you are.

'Darling, I wish you were here; you might be able to think of something. I'm really quite alarmed because I don't see how I'll ever get rid of her. I can't sack her in this condition and besides no one else will employ her, if they know she's pregnant. And it's three months already; she's put off telling me as long as possible in the hope this wretched man would take her to live with him. And you know she's a Catholic, too, and won't hear of abortion, so that's out, though God knows I'd be willing to pay, more than willing, delighted.

'Darling, I know it's awful to burden you with all this when you must have enough with your poor friend going mad and all the ghastliness of Essex, but you don't think, do you, that Erin might take her when her Swedish girl goes? I mean, would one more baby more or less make all that much difference to her household? I know I'm being selfish and I certainly wouldn't turn her out now; I imagine she'd have to go to one of those ghastly mother and baby homes or whatever they're called, where they make them scrub floors at six in the morning and tell them how wicked they've been. Or have I read the wrong newspapers? But afterwards, when she's had it, what on earth will I do with a screaming infant in the flat? I mean it's quite bad enough, just another six months with all this crazy food and her smashing things right and left, and I expect that will all get worse, I'm prepared for that. But afterwards? Well, she's

66

bound to come back here, isn't she, if she's got nowhere else to go, and she'll be even less use to me then than she is already if she's always having to feed and change it. I'll end up looking after her or getting someone else to look after us both, and that's the height of insanity. Besides there just isn't *room*, not to mention my nerves. I had a wild moment when I thought I could send her back to Italy but she says her family would kill her and how do I know they wouldn't? And there are ten of them already, anyway, and they're terribly poor and respectable.

'So, darling, do try to think of something and maybe you could write to Erin; it might be better than me ringing her up. At least she would feel free to say no to you, though please God she won't. I've worked through all the people I know and I really can't think of anyone as . . . well, flexible as Erin, who's also at the same messy stage. I'd be so happy to compensate her for her trouble, that goes without saying, if she agrees.

'On the other hand, darling, I really don't want you to get too involved with my problems, when you have enough of your own, and certainly not to the exclusion of your work. That "Sex in Marriage" thing should be fascinating, and I hope you use all the lovely quotes I gave you, and as for the "Me and My Work", don't worry about that for a second, you know you can do that standing on your head, only don't say too much or they'll think you're conceited. However, I expect you'll make it funny and if you do that you can get away with murder. The English will accept anything if they think you have a sense of humour' (my mother is Irish, originally, well, more or less, as far as I can discover) 'which is quite absurd of them but there you are. They simply distrust people who take themselves seriously, and I never really know if this is healthy or neurotic.

'Darling, I'm glad of a chance to write to you – maybe you should go away more often, though God forbid – because I do feel that I didn't say nearly enough about *The Sabbatical Marriage* when I read it. The telephone is so hopeless and when I'm face to face with you I'm so proud of my clever daughter that I can't say anything at all about your work and anyway we always have so much else to talk about; such as men and all that lovely rubbish. But you captured so exactly the spirit and not the substance – and I know you didn't set out to write a biography of Daddy and me, that goes without saying – but it was all there, the spirit of it, in a lovely golden glow, in fact it made me cry, darling, in parts. I'll show you which parts when you come back. Did we really make you as happy as that? I do hope so, because that was our intention, only intention is the wrong word, it was simply part of the general pattern, intention sounds much too deliberate, whereas happiness just evolves out of rightness.

'I think your style has improved enormously, not that I didn't adore the other two, you know I did, and I shall always treasure that outraged letter your ex-headmistress wrote me about *World* (poor soul), she had a moustache if I remember rightly), but in *S-M* you are so much more disciplined and economical. I expect the child narrator was a help : this probably demanded an extreme simplicity which is both natural and artificial at once. It fascinates me, darling, it really does, to see the way in which each book dictates its own form. I know this is vital and integral and I do try to see it in other people's books, really I do, only it shows most clearly in yours. I think this makes you a true artist, darling, because it's an instinct, like wearing the right scent for the right man, and it can't be taught or learned from experience so in a way it's even more important than insight or character or style. I also wanted you to know how touched I was by the dedication because I know how hard it is to dedicate a book to anyone after you've torn it out of yourself, like naming a child after someone else when it's yours and yours alone. Now I'm going to say something useless and I know I shouldn't, but I wish so much that your father had been alive to read it because he'd have been so proud. I've been thinking about him so much lately, particularly since this trouble with Maria, and I know I don't have to explain to you that this is not a utilitarian response.

'Darling, I think Lucrezia is going to have kittens again. I know she got out at the wrong time and now there is a most ominous bulge. Poor love, her inside will be quite worn out and it's all my fault. I know the vet thinks I'm mad, but I can't bear to spoil her fun and I always seem to find someone to take them eventually, though God knows it's touch and go at times.

'How is your poor friend – Christine, is it? I think I met her : a pale girl with lots of hair? Can you bring her back to town for a rest? She must be worn out with those children and no help; I thought of myself when you told me about her and how I would have gone out of my mind without Eileen when you were small. Do try to bring her back with you in any case because I am quite worried about you out there. It's all fields and cows, isn't it, and I believe when you get to the sea it's just a nasty little inlet; have you had a look yet? I can't imagine you being happy there even for a week and I'm most concerned about how you'll manage to work. Can you get anything done with those children round you and nowhere to go for a walk? It really is a most unfortunate time to be away, not that there ever is a good time, but you've already missed Janet's first night and she was fantastic. The play wasn't much, unfortunately, but she was tremendous and there was such a nice party afterwards. She sends her love, anyway.

'Darling, do get this month's *Queen* if you can – do they sell it out there? Because there is a most lovely cover of Catherine. Really, she gets more beautiful all the time; I couldn't be more lucky in my daughter-in-law if I had chosen her myself. I'll never forget how Peter walked in with her and I didn't even know she existed and he said, "We're engaged," just like that. I nearly fell on my knees in gratitude; it seemed quite inadequate to embrace her. They are all well, and the children are blooming; he's up to his eyes in work and loving every minute of it, and Catherine isn't pregnant again, thank God, (I forgot to tell you we had a little scare, you were so busy with Robert's departure) but planning to do some modelling in Paris, which will be lovely for her. Really, I'm so lucky in my children, I couldn't be prouder of you all. It really must prove something about life, although God knows what, when everything turns out so beautifully.

'Darling, I will have to stop any minute as Carlo is calling for me and I must change. He's very sweet; I think you'll like him. We must have a big party when you get back. I hope you have had lots of letters from Robert already; I won't tell you not to miss him too much because that's inevitable and probably quite good for you. I like him so much, although he's quite wrong for you on a long-term basis; however that doesn't matter, you must just live from day to day like all of us now, until your turn comes. I've had mine, of course, but yours is still out there waiting for you, and you can't hurry it, only move towards it at a normal pace.'

There followed a paragraph about clothes and the letter ended as usual with love and a cluster of big childish kisses. I cried. I had taken my mother's letter up to my room as a treat, which I knew it would be, and I cried. My mother is so valuable a commodity that I feel she should be shared out among the impoverished; I feel I am selfish and over-privileged to have so much of her for my own private consumption. I was pleased with the news of Catherine, who is my brother's wife and incredibly beautiful, with huge golden eyes and a small cat's pointed face, and masses of straight blonde hair, like a Swedish film-star, hanging right down past her shoulders and fringed above her eyebrows. Physically she is the same type as Lucas but infinitely more delicate and small-boned so that side by side with her (a situation both avoid) she would make Lucas look like a milk-maid. But it is not even her beauty that is the remarkable thing about Catherine, nor her huge, healthy children who, it seems, cannot possibly have emerged with such ease from that narrow and exquisite body, nor the fact that my incredibly sweet and conventional brother succeeded in marrying her. The thing that rivets and compels my fascinated attention is her extraordinary stillness and silence. People talk of hostile silence and companionable silence, but I have never felt either with Catherine. Silence with her belongs to a completely different order : it is like a perfume created specially for her and she moves serenely in its aura.

So I rejoiced for Catherine and her picture in *Queen*, her modelling prospects in Paris, and my mother's pride in her. I rejoiced without malice or envy. But still I wept. For my mother's letter was too much, just as my mother is too much, for me to bear. At least in my present state of deprivation. It brought it all back, the smell of the city, the news of our shared friends, our mutual concern. My mother gives so much that nothing less than total involvement is a fitting response. And here was I exiled from her, condemned to letters or at best (least?) the telephone. For my mother, with her overwhelming talent for people and feelings, has crashed the parent-barrier and emerged as a person, even a friend. Perhaps most of all as a friend. And so separation from her is painful.

I re-read the letter. I am sufficiently self-indulgent and masochistic to do this. I exercised my mind over Maria's predicament and Erin's possible co-operation. (Poor Erin.) I soaked myself in the praise of *The Sabbatical Marriage*, as in a long, hot bath, for complete approval and comprehension are rare and therefore precious. My mother is so ideal that she might be an invention: it is as if someone had drawn up a blueprint of a perfect mother especially for me. So I wept with sheer nostalgia and was unashamed. She had told everything and asked everything; as a complete person she wrote complete letters, and not with any sense of obligation but for her own satisfaction and out of her own nature. I wanted to be with her. I wanted to be in London again. I wanted my own flat.

I opened the window and breathed the chill, pure air. I peered into the gloom of the brown fields and the green fields. And I thought of Christine, who had retreated that day, the fatal morning after, into conventional retirement: 'I got awfully drunk last night, Alexa; I'm afraid I talked a lot of nonsense.' And I had said the only possible thing: 'I don't remember, love; I was pretty drunk myself.' But I did remember, and I was depressed. Not only for Christine's life and self-revelation, though that was sad enough, but for the fact of her withdrawal, and the necessity for it. I hate meanness and fear, whether in sex or conversation; people should be able to give and take freely and willingly at the time without an aftermath of regret and embarrassment. I learnt this so early from my mother that it has long been second nature, and even on the rare occasions when the consequences are disastrous, I do not care, because it still seems to me the only real way to conduct relationships.

I wanted to telephone my mother immediately, but I did not feel I could speak freely on Christine's phone, nor run up a huge bill which she would probably refuse to allow me to pay. Nor did the idea of the local call-box, even if it were in working order, appeal to me much, with its necessary pile of small coins, dictating a foresight and calculation of which I am hardly capable. And even if these objections had not existed, I would have still wondered if the sound of my mother's voice, with all its sympathy and interest, were not a luxury I could ill afford, as her letter had already produced the most painful nostalgia. But I felt, all the same, the identical homesick self-pity and sense of isolation I had experienced once in Yugoslavia when I was ill and alone and did not speak the language. There, too, there had been no one around the corner to visit, with whom proper communication was possible; my only link with the world outside, my world, had been through the capricious continental telephone.

So I did not telephone; and besides, I knew that there would be a prompt reply to my own distressed letter and I was fairly content to wait for it. Instead, I resigned myself to watching the progress of the ensuing week (for everyone seemed to assume that I would sit around idly waiting for some decision to be made). There seemed a definite policy of retrenchment in evidence : our evenings, which, after the first drunken orgy, had been vaguely occupied with Scrabble and Television, were now given over to strange three-cornered conversations in which Paul and Christine seemed to unite to demonstrate, through carefully selected trivia, the underlying strength of their marriage; and yet, before this process could go too far, Christine would suddenly change sides and join me, as if to show him that we had more in common than he wanted to think. I became fascinated by the entire game and tried to remember snippets of it to write down in my room.

C.   Alexa told me Lucas has had another abortion.
P.   Oh, really. She was one of your group, wasn't she?

C. Yes, she's a model. She always was pretty unstable.

A. I know what you mean, Christine, but I don't think unstable is quite the word.

C. Well, amoral then. I mean she always had a peculiar sense of values.

P. It doesn't sound to me as if she has any values at all, except perhaps self-preservation.

A. That's a little unfair, Paul, when you don't know her.

P. (to C.) I expect Alexa thinks her friends can do no wrong.

C. (hotly) Alexa is a very good friend.

P. I'm not denying that. Do forgive us, Alexa, discussing you in your presence.

C. Then what?

P. (lightly) I'm just saying you should be grateful I rescued you from bad influences such as Lucas.

C. But she's a very sweet person. She was always so kind to me. Darling, you are ridiculous; you're picturing a wild fast set and it wasn't like that at all, was it, Alexa? (And later, about holidays :)

C. Do you remember that cottage we took in Wales, darling?

P. What, the one with no sanitation?

C. Yes, but it was lovely, wasn't it, apart from that? All those gritty sandwiches on the beach.

P. I remember trying to get Michael to go in the water.

C. Oh yes, he was so frightened at first, wasn't he, but afterwards he loved it.

P. I'm sorry, Alexa, this must be all very boring for you.

A. Why should it be?

P. Well, I expect you're used to hearing about more exotic holidays.

C. Darling, you are silly, what's wrong with simple pleasures? (Laughing.)

P. Nothing, especially if they're all you can afford.

A. Good God, you talk as if I were Rockefeller at least.

P. Well, by our standards you probably are, near enough.

C. Oh Paul, why do you have such a complex about money?

The trouble here is that the best examples were not the ones I remembered : the best were too subtle and faded in the course of the evening, and certainly before I could get upstairs to my notebook. But the flavour was unmistakable : a controlled hostility alternating with possessive alliance, and they were bouncing this strange substance off me instead of each other. I was rapidly becoming a pawn in their game (strange how tension leads to mixing of metaphors) and this was ironic in the extreme when I basically prefer to make things happen – or to escape. Here I was not allowed to do either.

One evening I sat listening in trepidation for cries I would not know how to soothe, while Paul and Christine went to the pub. Another evening she and I went while he stayed with the children. But our conversation was general and she seemed rather eager to point out the village quaintness of everything and the rural friendliness of the people. The message was clear : it is not as bad as I made out; you must forget what I said. I was upset that she felt it necessary to do this with me but I accepted it with a kind of numb resignation. On another evening, she insisted on staying at home and urged Paul to take me to the pub. I dreaded what this might provoke but it was mercifully crowded and we shouted banalities at each other above the general uproar.

Christine during this period combined violent activity with profound lassitude. I had begun to help her as much as I could around the house but none the less she plunged herself into domestic work as if therein lay salvation. In what free time she had, and which I increased for her, she gave a great deal of emotional attention to the children, not only playing with them a lot but picking them up most abruptly to hug them and kiss them, often when they were absorbed in something else and quite put out by a sudden display of affection. 'I shall miss them, you know,' she said to me once, and there were tears in her eyes so I could not ask if she had actually made up her mind to go. This was ironic and amusing, since her decision was of some importance to me.

About halfway through the week we had our only significant conversation. We were in the kitchen, where she seemed to find it easier to talk while her hands were busy and could provide her with punctuation or distraction. She had been asking me what I was working on now and I took the easy way out by giving her my notes to read, though I would not, of course, have shown her the actual typescript, upstairs, on which I was gradually imposing some kind of order.

I watched her while she read and some of the quotes she was reading moved through my mind. 'I try to pretend he's someone else to make it more exciting – anyone. Like a film star, maybe, or an old boyfriend. I don't think that's cheating, do you? Not if it makes it better for both of us, and as long as he doesn't know. Well, it can't hurt him, can it?' And another : 'I really dread it now, because it's always the same. I know all the movements in advance, all the stages, and exactly how we'll end up. Even when he says let's do that for a change, I know what sort of change it'll be. So what's the point? I end up pretending I'm tired or I have a headache so we won't have to bother. I get so detached when we do it, I anticipate every movement. It's rather like dancing.' And the other side of the picture : 'If only we did it more often. I keep hoping we will, but he doesn't even watch me now when I'm getting undressed. He always used to and I liked that but now he's always got his nose in some book. I don't think he sees me any more, not properly. Oh, I know I could suggest it and maybe that's what he wants, but I can't, I want him to come after me.' Or else : 'It's this wretched climate. I keep thinking if only we could make love in the garden or something but there are the neighbours, aren't there, and at night it's so cold. But maybe even that would be better; maybe we're too comfortable in the house. And it nearly always happens in bed when I just want to sleep. I keep thinking about grass.' And another, more organized : 'I've got it all worked out now. Well, you have to, don't you? I mean I think, well, I've got the children and the house, I mean I've got what I wanted, and he works very hard so if he still wants it, well, he's entitled, isn't he, that's my part of the bargain. Well, it is a bargain, really, isn't it, when all's said and done?'

I had been amazed, as always with journalism, by how freely people talk once initial shyness wears off. Some, of course, won't let you record or make notes at first but mostly after ten minutes or so they're so carried away by what they're saying, so fascinated by themselves, that they don't seem to notice you scribbling away. They certainly don't seem to mind. But I should not be surprised at all, for television documentary has made such inroads into privacy, and people, both famous and ordinary, have gone along with it so wholeheartedly, that the anonymity of print is positively secretive by comparison.

Some of my best quotes, of course, come from Erin and Lucas and my mother, regular interviewees for almost any subject. I do not feel it is cheating at all to draw again and again on my friends because they are fascinating people and I am after high-quality material; moreover, I know they will be real with me and not put on an act. However, I did not submit their remarks to Christine: an odd piece of reticence, I thought, when they would finally be printed for the whole world to see.

'Well,' she said at last, 'that just about covers everything, doesn't it?', and I could not tell which part had impressed her most. I tried.

'It's sad,' I said. 'The way so many of them find it goes stale. That's always worried me about marriage. There ought to be some way to keep the original excitement.'

Christine did not look at me but started mixing something in a bowl. She said, 'I suppose you've never lived with anyone long enough for that to happen,' and I could not tell whether she sounded envious or derisive.

'Well, no,' I said. 'I haven't. Not yet.'

There was a long pause, full of wooden spoon clanking on earthenware. Then she said, 'I suppose that's the price you pay for your free life, not to know about marriage. Anyway—' She spoke slowly, as if the words were being dragged out of her – 'it's not so much stale, as ... different. It changes. It gets deeper and different. And children make a difference, I think.'

She had used the word so often that I thought she must be very struck by the contrast between past and present. I said, 'What did you think of the woman who said changing partners occasionally helped?'

I had never seen Christine blush, it occurred to me, but now there was an unmistakable pinkness creeping up her neck and over her cheeks. 'Oh,' she said, making it a long word. 'I didn't understand that at all. I think that must be so destructive.'

'But she said it worked for her,' I insisted. The woman had impressed me, I remembered her well. So jolly and domesticated, making cakes for her children at the time of the interview, her image quite at variance with her information.

'Well, she'd hardly admit it had been a disaster,' said Christine quite sharply.

'No,' I said. 'She probably wouldn't have mentioned it at all. So the odds are it's true.'

'Oh, I don't know.' Christine shrugged. 'I think it's like all those sex surveys, like Kinsey and people. I think everyone likes to exaggerate. I think some play it up and some play it down; I don't see how you ever get at the truth.'

I said, 'Yes, I know. I agree with you, up to a point. But sometimes a lot of truth shows through the lies people tell. Don't you think?'

Christine was silent for a long time. At last she said with an air of finality, 'I don't know, Alexa. I don't know at all. That's more your territory than mine.' And though she smiled to soften the words, the warning was clear.

13

So it was, I suppose, unfortunate that I was working on that particular feature then. In London, with Robert around, it was fun compiling notes and discussing them; there was no strain involved. (And the other feature, the one on work, merely fed my ego.) But here, trying against odds to concentrate on this particular subject, I was like a man on a health-farm trying to write about food; and worse, on a health-farm where the other inmates were on a higher calorie diet. I began to realize that my lack of attention to work had not been sheer laziness: Paul and Christine actually disturbed me. I was not used to being in a deprived position and it seemed that the fact of their physical relationship came between me and my work. I wondered in fact if my mother had this in mind when she wrote. She answered my SOS promptly, as expected, with a note simply saying, 'Don't worry, I'll think. Letter follows.' And a letter did follow, full of diplomatically-phrased misgivings about my entire situation. But worse, it coincided with the first of the many letters she hoped in vain I had already had from Robert, and a letter from Robert, though God knows how much longed for, was the least useful thing I could have.

Robert's letters are short. Like many writers, myself included, he is generally so involved in work or in recovery from work, that he resents putting pen to paper in a non-professional capacity. His letters are few and seldom run to more than two pages, at least one of which is devoted to explaining why the letter cannot be longer. But the second page usually makes up for this by describing in the most exquisite erotic detail what we would be doing if we were together. For Robert is an artist in four-letter words from both sides of the Atlantic: his love scenes are the best things in his misbegotten novel, he elevates pornography into art, and he is the only man I have ever known who can virtually give me an orgasm over the phone. So I read his letter over and over again, the second page, after the brief data on New York and his mother and his reasons for brevity, and I heard his voice as I read, the words sprang off the page and went straight to their target. I read and I read, and tormented myself. And Christine chose this very evening to curl up on the couch with extreme inertia and say firmly to Paul, 'Darling, it's such a lovely evening, why don't you take Alexa for a drive; you could go to the sea.'

I protested at once, though the word sea, even in the circumstances, even knowing it was the 'nasty little inlet' my mother had described, and knowing it meant being in the car with Paul, worked on me its usual magic. 'Oh no,' I said. 'Why don't you go? I can go to the sea any time. You two go and I'll baby-sit.' And I knew as I said it that I was probably condemning myself to a lonely, masturbatory evening.

But Christine smiled her most beguiling smile, which makes her look fifteen at the most, and said, 'Love, I couldn't. It's sweet of you but I couldn't move. I'm so tired. I just want to vegetate and watch television. You two go. Do take her, Paul, she's hardly been out at all since she came.'

Paul, too, seemed in an exceptionally good mood, and smiled at me pleasantly. 'Well, I'd certainly like some sea air,' he said. 'How about it, Alexa? Are you coming?'

I gave up. I knew I would go. The sea, in any form, is irresistible, and besides I am a shade fatalistic: if people push me so far I believe that the destination is unavoidable and I cease to struggle.

'Sure,' I said. 'You just talked me into it.' And I went upstairs to change into something more suitable for clambering over rocks, should there be any rocks. I looked at myself in the mirror for a long moment and I thought I looked odd: I did not try to interpret what I saw.

We left, Christine waving us goodbye with a limp hand.

The front door slammed behind us with curious finality; but then I always tend to feel on leaving anywhere that there is at least a chance I may not return. This is presumably a desire for uncertainty pushed to its most extreme form. We climbed into the old Ford, whose doors closed with difficulty; it was full of toys and old shoes and bags of sweets and cigarette cartons, and its paint was rusty and chipped. I settled myself in discomfort and Paul got in.

Eventually, it started. We both said nothing while he was struggling with it, but when it finally started and I could breathe with relief that we were spared the final indignity of being physically unable to go, he said, 'Poor old girl. I'm afraid she's not what she was.'

I said lightly, taking my cue from him, 'Well, none of us are,' as we nosed our way down the lane and onto the road.

'I got her for fifty pounds,' he said, 'and that was four

years ago. Spent another fifty on her and she still goes, just about. So I suppose I got a bargain.'

'Yes,' I said. 'I suppose you did.'

'She needs a bit doing to her now,' he went on. 'But she'll have to wait.'

I said nothing. Around us, on either side of the road, the flat Essex fields extended themselves to infinity in the pale, dying sunlight of a spring evening.

'I'm sorry,' he said. 'I expect I'm boring you.'

'Not exactly,' I said. 'There's just nothing I can say. I don't know about cars. But I don't mind listening.'

'You're very polite.' He seemed more grateful than ironic, for once. The boyish charm was uppermost, I thought rather apprehensively. 'The car's a sort of hobby really, I suppose. When I first got her, you know, I was pretty pleased with myself. And even now I like . . . well, tinkering about with her.'

'Yes,' I said. 'Of course.'

'Well, there's nothing much else to do round here,' he said, a shade defensively. 'I'm lucky, of course; school keeps me pretty busy. But it's a bit boring for Chris. That's why I always hoped she'd take up her music again. But she hasn't. She hardly touches the piano these days. In fact she doesn't even play records any more.'

I wondered how far it was ethical for me to discuss my friend with her husband. The other way round, of course, is always fair game. 'I think,' I said hesitantly, 'she hates being reminded of how good she used to be.'

He sighed. 'Oh, she always was a perfectionist, I know that. It makes life pretty difficult for her.' (But I felt he meant rather for all concerned.) 'She's still pretty good, though, you know, when she bothers with it.'

It seemed I was bound to be sucked into this conversation, ethics or not. I said, 'I don't think it's a question of bothering. I'm sure she's pretty good still; she must be. But I don't think she can bear to be less than the best. And she was the best, you know, Paul; or she would have been. She was pretty fantastic.'

I must have annoyed him for he accelerated and we nearly hit a small animal scurrying across the road. Paul swore and apologized.

'That's all right,' I said. 'It survived.'

'Yes, I know. But it would have been my fault if it hadn't. I'm sorry. You're quite right about Chris. But I realized that long ago. I do know her quite well, after all.'

'Yes, of course. You're married to her.'

'I'm sorry,' he said. 'I'm being touchy and ridiculous.'

Apology is always disarming. I remember how my mother tried to impress on me that the one who apologizes first is usually rewarded by a position of strength; I always mean to try this more often.

'It's just that you remind me,' he said, 'and I'm sure you remind Chris, of everything she's given up. But for me and the kids she could have had a great career. That's about the size of it, isn't it? Go on, be honest, admit it.'

I said, 'I think so. As far as anyone can tell. These things are so uncertain.'

'Oh, come off it,' he said irritably. 'Now you're giving me the party line. A minute ago you said she would have been the best.'

'All right,' I said. 'That was just my opinion. Okay. But I can't guarantee she'd have had a great career.'

'I'm sorry,' he said again. 'I must feel guilty, I suppose, or I wouldn't be so defensive.'

Honesty, like apology, has an irresistible appeal. I said gently, 'Oh, forget it.'

'That's just it,' he said. 'I can't. Particularly since this baby business. Particularly since you came. I'm sorry, Alexa, I'm not accusing you of anything, it's not your fault. But you must be honest with me or there's no point in talking. Do you think Chris is wasting her life?'

As soon as he said it I realized the question had been inevitable: it had been hovering unspoken around us ever since my arrival. And I believe, God knows, in honesty. But I could not see how it would help us. So I said, 'Paul, I honestly don't think I can answer that. I know it sounds corny but ... well, one person's waste is another's fulfilment, surely. Okay, Christine's wasting her talent as a pianist, but she's using other talents instead ...' I paused. It actually *was* corny.

'As wife and mother,' he said bitterly and pompously.

I sighed and shrugged. The car, which was small, seemed even smaller; we were claustrophobically enclosed in this tiny space, staring straight ahead and analysing Christine's life. Even the great flat wastes of countryside around us took on the guise of a refuge. I longed to jump out of the car, and began to wonder at what speed one would actually break a leg as opposed to receiving what are generally called abrasions.

'Yes,' he said. 'Exactly. I gave her a choice, not in so many words, not deliberately even, but that's what it amounted to. A plain, old-fashioned choice. So much for the emancipation of women.'

I said nothing. He seemed wound up anyway and I thought he would go on without prompting.

'It's ironic,' he said, 'because I don't think either of us realized at the time. There simply wasn't any question of choice : she was going to go on. You know that concert she did the first year we were married.'

'Yes,' I said. 'It was marvellous. And she got fabulous notices for it, didn't she?'

He did not seem to be listening. 'It could all have gone on from there,' he said. 'She even enjoyed the teaching side, I think, in between. But then my father died and Chris was pregnant so we had to move ... Still, even then we still thought ...' A long pause. 'No. Perhaps not any more after that. Strange how suddenly everything closed in. Like this place, in a way.' He took a hand off the steering wheel to wave at the view. 'There's a word for it, isn't there? Lowering, I think.'

'Yes,' I said softly. 'That's probably it.' The light was going, very slightly, even as we drove.

'I think about it at school sometimes,' he said. 'When I'm trying to get the kids to appreciate their surroundings. Uphill work, really, and I feel pretty dishonest at times.'

I said, 'Do you hate living here?'

He shrugged as we turned a corner. 'Oh, hate's a strong word. I grew up here; there are so many ties. You don't love a place for what it is but for what it's given you – at least that's what I think. And this place is all mixed up with my childhood and school and going to Oxford. So I don't think I can judge. I suppose in a way I love it, though I certainly don't think it has much to recommend it – intrinsically, that is. But that's all very well for me. It's not fair to inflict it on Chris.'

I said, 'I don't think you should worry too much about that. I don't think she hates it. I mean, apart from London, I don't think there's anywhere else she'd particularly like to be.'

'Oh, I know that,' he said at once. 'But that's just acceptance, isn't it? Not very positive.' He paused. 'We used to go out, you know. When we first got the car, before Michael was born. We used to just drive around. It sounds pretty pointless, I know, but it was fun.'

'Yes, of course.'

'Anyway,' he said. 'We don't do that much now. It's not easy to get sitters and Chris doesn't like the people here much. Oh, I don't blame her.'

We drove on in silence. I waited for more. I am always pleased with the role of listener; it is usually more rewarding, for, after all, I know about myself. But this time it was also uncomfortable.

'But it's a burden, you know,' he went on quite suddenly. 'Have you ever thought what a burden it can be to know how much someone has given up for you?'

I thought about this; it seemed painfully heartfelt. 'I can imagine,' I said, 'of course, that it must be a burden. But I can't say I know. Because no one has ever given anything up for me.'

He said grimly, 'You're lucky.'

I said, 'Well, it works both ways. I've never given up anything for anyone either. I just don't believe in sacrifice. I think it makes the giver feel resentful and the recipient feel guilty. I think it's unhealthy. So I never expect anyone to make sacrifices for me because I'm not prepared to do it for them.'

'Ah,' he said. 'You're very wise. But people don't always wait to be asked.' We then drove in silence for a while until he said, 'However, you've made your position clear. You would never, for instance, give up your career – say if you got married?'

83

I was truly amazed : such a thing had never entered my mind. I said, 'That would be like giving up breathing. I might as well be dead; I wouldn't exist.' But I remembered then, quite suddenly, how Robert, one bitter evening, had said to me, 'You care more about your work than about me,' and I had tried to argue that the conflict was non-existent, like a clash between eating and sleeping, or else absurd, like the old childish game of would you rather be blind or deaf if you had to be one or the other, would you rather lose an arm or a leg? But he had insisted, and refused to see it, and in the end I had been driven to say, as I now said to Paul, that if I couldn't work I might as well be dead because I would not be me as I knew myself, which surely is a definition of death (i.e. non-existence) and that as a writer himself he must see this, because it must be the same for him. But the evening had ended badly.

'In other words,' Paul said, 'you can't imagine loving anyone that much.'

I said, 'But it's not a question of love, it's a question of capacity.'

'Is it?' he said. 'Then you mean your capacity for love is limited.'

I had not meant this at all but I wondered now if it might be true. It sounded unpleasant, though, when he said it, so in self-defence I ran over the people I knew, in my head, a rapid review. 'Perhaps,' I said, 'but then surely everyone's is. No one has an unlimited capacity for anything, even love.'

'If you really think that,' he said, and I detected a note of satisfaction as if I had fallen neatly into a well-laid trap, 'then you don't know Chris at all. Never mind. I've said quite enough already. We're nearly there.'

# 14

WE drove down what was almost a cart-track, lined on either side by bungalows with names such as Sea-view and Mon Repos, and beyond them in a field a whole fleet of caravans. It was a desolate scene, mid-week and early spring; there was no-one about. Presumably the season had not yet begun.

I said, 'Where are we? What is this?'

Paul said, 'We're just beyond Burnham-on-Crouch, didn't you notice? It's such a picturesque name I thought it would strike you.'

The Ford bumped a little at the end of the lane and swung round into a field with a no-parking sign. We stopped and he switched off the engine. 'Here we are,' he said, pointing ahead. 'Behold the sea.' And I resented the words because they open the Vaughan Williams' Sea Symphony and he had brought the music pouring into my head and disturbed me. We both got out of the car and pressed the doors shut. A tiny, cold breeze was blowing and I looked out over the bushes and saw, indeed, the sea, enclosed almost entirely by curving land. I fixed my eyes on the narrow outlet in the distance through which one could sail, could escape, to the true ocean, to no horizon, to space. I felt sad. It was like seeing the sea in captivity, like a lion in the zoo.

'Come on,' said Paul. 'We might as well go on the beach now we're here.'

The beach was shingle. No sand. Our feet crunched on it and a few birds made sounds and the wind moved the bushes but otherwise there was silence, total lonely silence, the silence of desolation. I thought it was the loneliest spot I had ever seen in my life. But the water was there, and it moved, just a little; it lapped at our feet. And there were a few bits of seaweed and driftwood and stones, left stranded in a line by the miniature tide.

'It's so quiet,' I said, and found myself whispering.

Paul said in a normal voice. 'You should see it in summer. In another month even. In May when the season begins. The bungalows back there are just week-end places mostly, but the caravans fill up with trippers; the whole place is over-run. You can hardly move for people.'

'I can imagine,' I said. But I couldn't. It had the air of a place that was permanently uninhabited, a lost, forgotten place, that would never be crowded or warm. In a sense it was beautiful, even; at the same time alarming. As Lucas would have said, a good spot for a murder; she has an eye for the macabre.

'I used to come here in winter a lot,' Paul said. 'When I was a boy. It's at its best then, really icy. I used to walk up and down and throw stones at the sea and dream about the future. I was very ambitious then.' He laughed, rather bitterly. 'Yes, me.'

'Why not?' I said lightly, disturbed. 'We all were. It's an ambitious time, adolescence, isn't it, for everyone?' I thought of what Christine had told me, about his wanting to write, and I feared he would say too much and regret it later. I hate people to regret things.

'Oh yes, I suppose so,' he said. 'We all were, all three of us. But for you it came true. You're the only one. Chris and I had to settle for less.'

'I'm sorry,' I said inadequately.

'Don't be sorry,' he said. 'Chris enjoys your success; it means a lot to her.'

I said, 'Yes, I know. I realize that.'

'But I don't,' he said. 'In fact I resent it. There now, I've said it.'

'I don't mind what you say,' I said honestly. 'If *you* don't. Just don't feel awful tomorrow, that's all.'

'Oh, I probably will.' He was standing very close to me; I could see the minute bristles of a day's growth of beard. 'So what? What the hell? I'd like to feel a lot worse.'

I knew I should move; I knew what was coming. But we both seemed immovable, rooted in shingle, and the silence was so vast and the place so empty, that any move would have looked too large and significant; and to shift even a foot on the pebbles would have made a noise.

'God, you're beautiful,' Paul said softly. He put a hand on my cheek, the first time he had touched me except to shake hands, and I trembled inside because Robert's letter was still with me, raising the temperature of my very bones. 'You have yellow eyes like a cat,' he said, and suddenly kissed me. For an instant it was tentative, then immediately it took fire and blazed into mad give and take, as if we had to devour each other to survive. The whole thing was sensation entirely; I did not have a single thought, of guilt or surprise or joy, in my head. There was no room for thought of any kind. It went on for minutes or centuries, and he put one hand behind my head in a tangle of hair as if he needed to hold me, as if I were struggling to get away, and the other inside my coat : I felt it close on my breast for a second and the whole thing was too much for me, on top of Robert's letter and the past fortnight; my inside turned over and melted and I wanted to pull him down on the shingle and have him completely, there and then. And at that moment, of course, he stopped, bruising my mouth, as if he had to bite off the kiss to end it, and taking his hands away. I swayed a little on my feet with shock.

He murmured, more to himself than me, 'God, I want you,' and immediately turned his back on me, plunging his hands into his coat pockets and walking away. I watched him as he strode down the beach and it was suddenly like a film shot : the whole thing was unreal and contrived. I took cigarettes and a lighter out of my bag and lit one with difficulty, cupping my hands against the wind. I needed the cigarette very badly but I did not want it; I had the taste of Paul in my mouth.

I watched him still in the distance and tried to calm myself as the cigarette took over. It went straight to my head, like the first of the day after trying to give it up, and made me giddy. But I could judge the degree of my recovery by the way in which I ceased to shake. Presently I saw Paul turn and begin to walk back to me; I thought he looked rather beautiful, young and tall but a little hunched in his duffle coat. Otherwise I did not allow myself to think at all.

He came up to me slowly, just as I finished my cigarette and threw it away. He looked at me very straight and for a moment I thought he was going to hold out his hand like a schoolboy after a fight, though God knows who was meant to have won. But instead he made a small helpless gesture, slightly foreign in its eloquence, and stood still about a yard away from me. We looked at each other for a moment and neither of us spoke; then he said,

'What on earth can I say?'

I wanted to be tender, not brisk, but I did not dare. I was overcome with pity and fear and gentleness; I did not want to speak at all.

'Don't say anything,' I said. 'There's no need. Come on—' and I held out my hand to him in friendship; I could not prevent myself. 'Let's go back.' He took it after a moment's hesitation, squeezed it briefly, (sending the most alarming tremors through me) and let it go, like something hot.

'Yes,' he said. 'Yes.' And we walked to the car in silence, side by side but a little apart, not looking at each other any more.

But since we obviously could not drive the whole way back in such a silence, so heavily charged and giving the whole incident too great a significance, I began to talk. And since we equally obviously could not talk about ourselves or Christine or my work, for a variety of very good reasons, I fell back on the old stand-by, and asked him about *his* work. I thought I detected relief; at any rate he answered readily, and I asked more questions, and presently we were having a very nearly normal discussion, similar to the one on my first evening, about the educational system in general and his school in particular, the problems of teaching his subject, the relationships between pupils and teachers, and most of all staff-room politics. Mostly I just encouraged him to talk, for I felt he was more in need than I was of the distance that words can put between events, but occasionally I threw in the odd reminiscence of boarding-school, especially those from which I had been expelled, and once or twice I actually made him laugh. It made for a surprisingly pleasant drive, for all antagonism seemed to have vanished, and I found myself thinking, though quite without lust, that it might have been even better had we actually made love : I generally feel very peaceful and friendly towards my men afterwards, and there is nothing like sex (if successful, that is) for drowning any hostility or competitiveness that a man may have felt beforehand. But about the abortive incident itself I did not think at all, so concerned was I with promoting calm and goodwill and oblivion. I knew I would go over it later but currently other things were of more importance. So when we got back to the cottage I was not prepared to re-open the issue. But he stopped the engine and just sat there at the end of the lane in the gloomy ten o'clock dark, and said finally, 'Alexa.'

I said brightly, 'It was a lovely evening, Paul. Thank you.'

He said, 'Yes, it was. But there's something I must say to you.'

I said, 'Don't. I know all those things and it's all quite all right. Let's just go in.' And I tried the door handle of the car on my side but it was stiff and would not open.

He said, 'I'll do that. But I really do want to say – well, if Chris decides to go, of course you're free to withdraw your offer, that's obvious. Only if you feel you can stay, for her sake, then I just want to say that there won't be any question of a repetition . . .'

He was dreadfully embarrassed and I hate embarrassment: it is usually so unnecessary as well as uncomfortable. I said, 'Paul, I know that. I understand perfectly, honestly I do. It was lovely and meaningless and it's all forgotten, so let's go in.' And I tried the car door once again but it wouldn't work for me. So he leaned across me, as I had been dreading he would, and shoved it down hard, and it opened. We were now so close that I could smell his skin, we were almost touching, and the reassurances we had just given each other seemed suddenly the barest of lies. He turned his face towards me for a second and it had all the classic beauty I have described, perhaps even enhanced by the gloom. We looked at each other and I thought, This is crazy, if he kisses me again now I'm done for, and the house and Christine are only yards away. But he only said, 'God,' very softly, and the cold air came into the car as the door swung open. We both took great gulps of it and he moved away to his own side of the car and opened his door and we both got out quickly, with an air of resolution.

'I meant to stop somewhere for a drink,' he said in a remarkably normal voice as we walked down the lane. 'But I forgot. I'm sorry. Would you have liked that?'

'It's all right,' I said. 'We might have been stopped by a cop.'

And he said, for we had been discussing figures of speech in the car, 'That's assonance,' and I said, 'Why, yes, so it is,' and we both found this funny and were laughing as we reached the front door and heard the music. We both stopped and shut up; Paul froze with his key in his hand. I said in a whisper, 'Is it her or a record?' and we listened but could not tell. 'I don't know,' he said. 'It's one of her pieces but it could be a record,' and for a few seconds we listened to Mozart, crisp and plaintive, as we stood on the step in the chilly night air with the gloomy fields all around us. The music worked on me, casting its usual spell, till Paul shocked me by saying, 'Oh, come on, let's go in; we can't stand here all night waiting for a wrong note to prove something.' And as he put his key in the lock the music stopped, instantly.

We stepped into the hall with its familiar smell, and hung up our coats, and the transition was sharp, as if we had returned from some supernatural state to reality. We walked down the passage into the living-room and there was Christine, still curled up on the sofa exactly as we had left her, as if she had not moved all the time, and no clue to be had about the source of the music. I wondered if Paul would ask her but he did not and she smiled at us both and said, 'Did you have a good time?' The moment was frozen for a second, so I knew it would join the few that are imprinted on my memory like photographs; then it all dissolved abruptly into chatter about the sea and the cold and the need for coffee or a drink. Paul sat down and lit a cigarette, picking up a newspaper; Christine went into the kitchen to put on the kettle, and I poured some of my own Scotch, for I had recently been driven to buy another bottle. When Christine came back with the coffee she said, 'Yes, it's a pity it's not a good beach; when we take the children in summer they can't make sand castles or anything. Still, it's nice to be near the sea.'

I said, 'Yes, you're lucky,' because I suddenly, desperately wanted her to be, and she smiled and said, 'Yes, I am. Especially if I can have a week in town. I'm sorry I've taken so long to decide but I really would like to go. Is your offer still open?'

And what could I say but, 'Yes, love, of course it is.'

## 15

NOISE. Taxis. Porters. People. Fumes of traffic, hordes of pedestrians. Shops, cars, buildings. Smells: food, bodies, fuel, smoke. The leather smell of my taxi and the driver delighted, as well he might be, with a fare from Liverpool Street to World's End. I am naturally extravagant, I know, but even were I the greatest miser alive, there could be no better way of celebrating my return to civilization. Red London buses bearing magic numbers and the names of all the places I have missed, bearing posters of films I have not seen. Advertisements slapped on the walls, shouting their products; shops crammed with everything, and the wonderful mess of street markets. Newsvendors croaking and car horns blowing; noise and colour and dirt. I am back. It's all right. I'm here. And you, are you the same? But how did you manage without me? How dare you in fact go on when I am away? Didn't you even notice something vital was missing? Out of sight, out of mind, is that it? Then I must never leave you again or you may even presume to forget me; is that all our long love affair means to you?

I lean back in my seat and close my eyes; they ache a little already from my greedy efforts to take in too much. I am starved; I shall make myself ill if I gobble like this. But I open my eyes, I have to look again, and look and look.

(Okay, I don't care if I'm sick.) There are so many land-marks, some famous like Nelson, others known only to me, like cafés on a certain evening whose continued existence I must verify. For it might all have changed; they might even have moved things. I must look and be sure it is still my city. It seems all right, certainly, but I would like to check every inch of it, and I can't; I have only twenty-four hours, too little for even the most ambitious tourist. Oh, lucky, lucky people, ugly and beautiful, with your blank faces, pushing and shoving each other, with your prams and your dogs and your shopping; lucky people, jumping on and off buses at the lights, disappearing into the blessed tube, losing yourselves in its windy, rattling caverns, have you been making the most of it? Have you kept it warm for me, and do you even realize how lucky you are not to have been away?

Outside my flat I alight and pay, over-tipping absurdly and giving the driver such a huge smile that he must surely think I am mad and he's right. 'God, it's good to be back,' I cannot prevent myself saying, and he says, 'Where you been then?' and when I say Essex I can see his surprise as I knew I would. He drives off, puzzled and happy, and it is all I can do in my state of insane exhilaration not to plant a shiny lipstick kiss on the back of his retreating cab. For it's not every day you come home.

The sheer possessive joy of my own key in my own front door, and the lovely knowledge that no one will be there. (At this moment I doubt if I would even welcome Robert.) My flat, empty. Just mine, all waiting for me. I step into a litter of mail from people with no forwarding address: already I am in demand. But it's too soon to open them; I am not yet ready for that. I glance briefly through at the envelopes: my American publishers, an old schoolfriend (Eve), a couple of ex-boyfriends, a party invitation on a postcard (too late, I've missed it already) and a handful of bills. Not a bad little haul. But first I must inspect the flat, my own (rented) property. It's not in a mess, as I told Christine it was, nor does it need twenty-four hours to be prepared for her, as I said it did, nor do I need the extra clothes I am also supposed to have come back for. It's in beautiful order, just as I (and my daily) left it, but it's cold, so I switch on the heating immediately. Then I wander round looking at the rooms and stroking things. Three rooms k. and b. needn't take much looking round but they can if you do it with love. I give myself the luxury of falling into the middle of my own huge bed and lying there for a moment pretending I have just woken up. I go into my little office and stroke my big typewriter, the resident one, and the packets of paper beside it. I look out of the window at the houses and roof-tops and the people behind their separate windows; I look down at the traffic in the street. It never stops, thank God.

I start opening windows as the place warms up, to let out the staleness of absence, and I spray a little favourite scent in all the rooms to put my presence back everywhere, to make believe I have not been away. For smells are important, and now the flat smells of me once again. In the living-room I switch on the gramophone and my current favourite record blasts the room into life. I go into the bathroom and start running a bath, pouring in essence as the steam rises; I go on to the kitchen and begin to make coffee. While I wait for it to brew I sit on a stool and open my mail. The bills are not too huge, the two ex-boyfriends want to see me again, but one has just left for Portugal so I've missed him this time, Eve wants accommodation in June : she is in a mess with her husband and lover and wants a rest (so she says) from both of them, which means she probably wants to start something new, with me as her cover. My American publishers have just sold the paperback rights of *Golden Girl* for quite a large sum to another American publisher who turned it down as a hard-back, and when, they say, oh when, is your agent going to send us your new book?

\*       \*       \*

I feel quite drunk by now with all this love and attention and reward; I actually need the coffee to sober me, it is no longer a simple urge to self-indulgence in smell and taste as it began. But I remember my bath just in time, a fraction before it becomes too full to accept both me and the water.

I can do with it deep. I want to wash every speck of Essex off myself, and bathing in Christine's chilly little bathroom has not been enough. In the bath I remember the hairdresser: I must phone and bully or charm him into a rapid appointment today or tomorrow. Two weeks of attending to my own hair have left the usual result and no matter if nobody notices but me, it is none the less real and depressing. And there are so many other people, to phone, and whom shall I see? For whom shall I try to look beautiful?

My preoccupation with the telephone now makes it ring (or so I would like to believe). I leap out of the bath, grab a towel, and run dripping across the hall. I adore the telephone as Jane Austen adored a knock on the door: it is the 'usual period of suspense' that I value most. The uncertainty is so delicious that I never object to the interruption, except when I'm working and sometimes not even then, if I'm stuck. And here the call must be for me, whereas in Essex it was invariably not.

It's Erin. 'Oh, you're back,' she says in tones of most gratifying relief.

'Yes, thank God, Oh, Erin—' But I cannot go on; I hear my voice shake and I am amazed at the strength of my own feelings.

'Bad as that?' she says, concerned.

'Oh *yes*. Worse if anything. But it's not that exactly. It's – oh, it's so lovely to be back, the flat's so lovely and the streets and the river – oh, Erin.' I find I am nearly hysterical.

'Steady,' she says.

'Yes, all right. Steady. No, I can't. God, it's so marvellous to be back.'

'Well, I started writing to you,' she says, 'when I got your letter. Then I thought you just might be back so I rang.'

'Oh yes,' I say, enchanted. 'I'm so glad you did. Oh, the lovely, lovely telephone.'

'Look,' she says, the absurd way people always do on the phone. 'First things first. Are you back to stay?'

'Oh no.' I wish she hadn't reminded me. 'Only for twenty-four hours. Oh, God. I'm only out on parole.'

'Then Christine is coming?'

'Yes. When I get back.'

'Oh,' she says, and there's a long pause. 'Is that really wise?'

'No, it's not. It's anything but. Only I can't get out of it.'

Erin misses nothing. 'Do you really want to get out of it?'

'Yes, of course I do.' How vehement I sound. 'Oh, I don't know. Maybe not. The whole thing's too much. It's all boiling up; I don't think I can handle it.'

'Sounds irresistible,' says Erin, who knows me so well. 'For you, I mean. I'd run a mile myself.'

'Yes, I know. I must be out of my mind.'

'Not at all,' she says, cynical and indulgent both at once. 'You'll probably get a book out of it. Or at least a short story.' For Erin and I work in completely different ways: she starts with pure fiction and moves towards fact; I am triggered by fact and advance into fiction. Erin finds herself, as it were, by writing about other people. I begin with myself and move outwards into unknown territory.

'I don't know about that,' I say, disturbed because the thought had of course crossed my mind and it is the calculating part of myself I like least. 'More likely a nervous breakdown. But how about you, how's your book?'

Erin is writing her fourth novel currently. (I shall probably never catch her up and I don't really care, though we like to play a game of gentle competition. She is older than I am though, so I suppose that makes it all right.) It's about a girl who thinks she has a vocation: at first she resists it and then she gives in and has a fight with her family and boyfriend, etc., and eventually goes in the convent. But they find out she hasn't a vocation, and she resists this, too, but eventually has to admit it and come out, and all the people who wanted to stop her going in are quite cross with her for coming out because they find it embarrassing to explain, like a broken engagement. And each time, going in and coming out, she has a terrific struggle to rethink her ideas about the world and about God. It's absolutely enthralling, though in anyone else's hands it would be corny; Erin let me read the first draft simply because she thought it was also the last, as usual. Then she changed her mind and decided it could all be better so she started again. I couldn't see why, but Erin is a perfectionist, so it probably *will* be better when she's finished with it. But the decision upset her because she's never had to write a book twice before.

'Oh, it's ghastly,' she says now. 'It's so awful it's just not true. I'm appalled that it's going to turn out a third rate carbon copy of *The Nun's Story* or *I Leap Over the Wall* or whatever it was called.'

'Nonsense,' I say. 'You know it won't. It was marvellous before, I told you that, so it can't be less than marvellous. Have you got a title yet?'

'No,' she says, the authentic voice of despair, so I know she is going to be flippant. 'The way it's going I might as well settle for "Carry on Postulant".'

I catch her mood, knowing she wants me to. 'How about "I crawl under the fence"?'

'That's it,' she shouts, delighted. 'That's it exactly. Oh, God.'

'No, but seriously,' I say, 'as they say. How far have you got?'

'Oh, not very far. That's the point. I'm still mucking about with her childhood. Only I'm trying to do it in flash-back but without letting it show, you know? So it's all in a muddle.'

'It'll get better.' Comfort is useless yet vital at times like this. It is all we can give each other : no one can help. The most solitary job in the world. 'It will, honestly. I promise you.'

'Oh, you're lovely,' she says, which is our way of saying we're fond of each other. 'But I don't know. I keep thinking I've really bitten off more than I can chew this time. I always knew I would eventually and I think this is it.'

'No, it's *not*.' She needs someone to be firm with her now. 'You're just not properly into it yet. Have you worked every day?' Erin goes to the British Museum to work, a mixed blessing, since sometimes she meets rather too many people all equally hung up on their novels and theses, and eager for coffee and chat. But at other times it works, and being, unlike me, a true academic, she enjoys the atmosphere and the physical nearness to so many of her old University haunts. For Erin at just twenty-nine has three children, three books and two degrees, facts which leave me permanently breathless and about which I never cease to boast to anyone who will listen. A year ago, before she was pregnant again, she was even going to write for *The Guardian* as well.

'No, I haven't,' she says. 'How did you guess? I've been doing it at home, or rather not doing it. Ingrid's got German measles and I'm sure all the kids will get it too, but in rotation, not together, of course. That's what I was coming to. This girl of your mother's . . .'

'Maria.'

'Yes. Well, I think I can take her. Simon says I'm crazy but if she doesn't mind sharing a room with the child when it comes, I think we can squeeze her in.'

I say, 'Oh, Erin, you are an angel.' I had known she would and I agree with her husband that she's mad. But I am delicately-poised loyalty-wise, as Robert would say, between Erin and my mother, and on balance Erin probably has greater reserves of sanity. 'She'll be so relieved,' I say. 'My mother, I mean.'

'Oh, she is,' Erin says. 'I 'phoned her. She was terribly grateful. But she didn't have much time to talk; she was just going away with someone.'

'Oh yes, Carlo.'

'No, I don't think so. Giovanni, I think she said.'

'Oh.' I'm surprised. Giovanni is a film-director with whom my mother has had an on and off relationship for years. 'I thought that was currently off.'

'Well, it must be on again. I think it was Giovanni. A longer name than Carlo, anyway.' Erin is inclined to be vague and my mother knows this, but she still assumes that everyone else shares my passionate interest in her affairs, simply because she does. It is this that makes her such a good friend : she gives the same degree of attention that she expects to receive. But my heart is sinking : my mother is currently inaccessible.

'Where's she gone?' I say. 'And for how long?'

'Paris, for a week,' says Erin, adding inevitably, 'I think. Don't be sad. I'm so sorry you just missed her.'

'Yes, so am I.'

'Oh, come on, Alexa, don't. How's work? There must be something cheerful. Have you heard from Robert?'

I tell her about Robert and my American publishers and the slow progress of the articles.

'Then we're both in the money,' she says jubilantly. 'I've won that silly prize, you know, the one they put me in for. Isn't it crazy? I'm quite knocked out, actually.'

Anyone else would have told me this first thing. 'Why?', I say. 'I knew you'd get it. How much?' But she doesn't know, of course; and being Erin she really doesn't know, she is not holding out on me.

'I thought I'd take Simon and the kids to Italy for a month,' she says. 'Your mother said we could borrow her villa. Isn't she sweet?' And she really means this, not seeing that my mother owes her anything. 'I thought in August, between Ingrid going and ... er, Maria coming. I've got hundreds of leaflets and things. Oh, Alexa, what are we doing on the phone? Why don't you come over and we could look at them together. Hey, why don't you come with us, too, it would be lovely.'

'German measles,' I say.

She sounds genuinely puzzled. 'Oh no, that'll all be over by August. Oh. I see. You mean tonight. Well, yes. Haven't you had it?'

'I'm not sure,' I say. 'Only my mother knows that. Anyway, can't you get it twice? Besides, I can't risk taking it back to Christine's kids.'

'Oh, no,' she says. 'Of course not. What a pity.'

'Anyway,' I say, 'I have to have a bath and get my hair done and phone everybody, and much as I'd love to see you, I also rather want just to be alone in the flat. It's so lovely to be somewhere that's mine again.'

'Yes, of course,' she says. 'I do see that. Maybe it's just as well. Simon's asked some people to dinner and I haven't even shopped yet, what with Ingrid and the kids and everything. I don't know what they'll eat. Still.' Erin loves the chaos of her life, only in her case it is domestic rather than emotional : she writes intense novels from a very calm standpoint. Simon is a bulwark against the world, charming and delightful : ideal for her but the last thing I would ever want.

When we hang up, at length, I go back to my bath, let cold out and hot in, and luxuriate. I get out, finally, and phone Alexis, who pretends at first to be cross and then says he can take me at ten tomorrow and I mustn't be late. We then have some silly chat about how much we've missed each other. Alexis is delightful, Russian and Cockney and madly queer; most of the gossip I hear comes from him. His salon is a temple of bitchery. But he is an excellent hairdresser and comparatively cheap. My father always taught me that having money is no reason to throw it around.

Now I am really at home again : my contacts have been re-established. Paul and Christine and the whole situation seem completely unreal. I sit and go through my address book. If only I had more time : it's agony. I am going to have to choose, and that means leaving something out. I want to walk all over London and peer into basements (it's amazing how many short stories spring up that way) but I also want to shop. I want to walk up the King's Road, my road, and go into a shop and listen to the music and buy a dress I emphatically do not need. I also want to phone my friends, all of them : Erin has only whetted my appetite for conversation. I want to see everyone; she has plunged me back into life, real life. My life. But there isn't time for it all, there isn't time for a quarter of it, and the pain almost chokes me. Moreover, I still look a mess and must do something about it, and I am also starving but do not want to cook or eat alone, and most of all, I want to make love. So it's a question of priorities. I go through my book again. There are people who will give me bed but not dinner, others who will give me dinner but not bed, and a select few, say half a dozen, who will, if not otherwise engaged, be very happy to provide me with both. But there is also Tony's letter. I scratched Tony out of my book because we broke up so violently; it was most unlike me but I did it. Now, however, I have his letter and his new phone number; and a voice from the past is irresistible. Particularly a voice I never thought I would hear again. For Tony has pride, and if Tony now crawls it is worth a lot. I let myself remember a little, just enough, to get into the mood. I dig out the right scent. Then I pick up the phone.

## 16

Tony says, 'Christ, how many times was it?'

I say luxuriously, 'I don't know. I lost track. Who's counting anyway?' I stroke his forehead, his eyebrows, his back. It's indescribably lovely to be hot and sticky and full and wet and used and exhausted and crushed and satisfied again. 'Lovely Tony,' I say appreciatively, as a form of shorthand.

He looks at me with the much too astute grey eyes I have almost forgotten. Now that his own spasms are over I can almost hear his brain start ticking again. 'Mm, maybe,' he says. 'I'd like to think so. But I get the feeling even the dustman would've done.'

I hug him tight, knowing he will come out soon and dreading the moment, and try flippancy to distract him from his theme. 'You *are* original,' I say. 'Why dustman? Most people would have said milkman.'

He comes out, and I can't help feeling he has picked that particular second just to punish me. I groan, and he ignores me, rolling over and lighting cigarettes for us both. 'I don't care for milk; I prefer dust. But you know bloody well what I mean.'

'Okay, okay,' I say. 'Don't spoil everything now. It was all so nice. I was pretty desperate, okay, and you were just what I needed.'

'Was I really?'

I know what he means and resent him for it. 'Well, you wrote to me,' I point out. 'I didn't sit here itching and think "Who shall I make use of? Ah, I know, Tony. He'll do." You wrote to me. And you haven't done so badly out of it yourself, admit it.'

'Oh, okay,' he says grudgingly. 'You've made your point. You're an aggressive bitch, aren't you?'

'Not at all. Only when provoked. And you provoked me.'

'Oh, come here.' And he pulls me round to face him and kisses me, a thoughtful, tasting kiss. 'Why didn't you write to me, incidentally?'

I feel a great surge of affection for him. We have been into all this, more or less, over dinner but it seems different in bed. 'Oh, I don't know. By the time all my scars had healed I was pretty involved with Robert and I knew you wouldn't like that much so there didn't seem any point in writing to you.' Tony likes the impossible in his girls : the exclusive nympho, the interchangeable sado-masochist, the versatile hetero-lesbian. We got along pretty well for about a year till he pushed his luck too far. That, come to think of it, was the only time in my life I was ever tempted to invoke the Law, until it occurred to me that it would simply add further pain, of a different variety, to what I had already suffered, while obliterating none of it. 'Come to that,' I say, 'why did you write to me?'

He kisses me again. 'Everyone else is away.'

'Sod.'

'Well. Shelley told me Robert had gone to New York and Lucas had gone to New York.' (Shelley shares a flat with Lucas and some of Tony's best photographs are of Shelley.) 'So I thought.'

'Yes. I see exactly what you thought.'

'Well? Isn't it so?'

'Oh yes. Almost certainly. But so what?'

'I see. Still the same Alexa.'

'It works both ways, Tony. I can be here now, for instance. And if Robert came back it wouldn't matter. But you're only here because he's away.'

'I don't like competition.'

'But it's not competition. It isn't as if either of you wanted to marry me, so what are you competing for?'

'I'm not. That's the point.'

'Oh, I *know* that. But if you were, I mean why use the word at all? There doesn't seem any clash at all to me. I'm only claiming the same rights to freedom as Robert has and you have and—'

He yawns to shut me up. 'Maybe I'm old-fashioned.'

'Oh, I see. The minute Robert gets back you'll disappear.'

'That's right.'

I don't know why I bother with this, only it's so nice to be in bed with Tony again and a lot of scars can fade in a year. 'But why?'

'You know why. I like all my girls sitting alone in their flats waiting for me to call them. I hanker for the good old days.'

'Tony, what good old days? There never were days as good as that. You either had to scratch around for it or pay for it, or else you got plenty because everyone else was getting plenty too. You're just not being realistic.'

'I need a harem,' he says contentedly, and pulls up the sheets. 'Christ, it's late. Can I stay the night?'

I hesitate. I am fussy about this : if not in love, there is a kind of extra pleasure about subsiding at last in one's own empty bed. But two weeks in Essex have made me lonely, and fonder of a human body next to mine in sleep. 'Oh, all right,' I say. 'Just this once.'

'That's what I like about you,' he says, 'always did. You're so generous.'

We don't speak for a while. I lie there realizing I have told him nothing about Essex and wondering if facts are seeping through my skin as we touch. It brings it all back, the time I lived with Tony, before I finally realized that I couldn't live with anyone, that they all, in one way or another, start to think they own you. There are too many areas for possessiveness : if it's not your body it's your mind or your money, your work or your friends. It's a pity, because it can be so lovely to come home to someone who cares about you, and for them to come home to you. But it always ends up with invasion of too many areas. People cannot, it seems, live together and yet keep their distance. Or perhaps this is simply another way of saying that men like my father are rare.

'Tony,' I say, quite suddenly out of a deep pit of sleep, surprising myself because I didn't know this was on my mind. 'Didn't you worry at all?'

'When?'

'You know.' I cannot bring myself to be specific : melodrama, taken to excess, always makes me self-conscious. 'Didn't you want to know how I was? Didn't it occur to you I might bleed to death or something?'

He actually laughs at this; he has a convenient memory. 'Don't be daft,' he says. 'I only scratched you.'

'Stitches,' I say. I have waited a year to tell him this. 'I had to have stitches.' I wonder if the pride shows in my voice.

'Oh well,' he says, close to sleep. 'They haven't left a mark. And now you know how it feels you can use it in a book.'

## 17

IN the morning I give him breakfast and throw him out, not without difficulty. He is in a mellow mood, typical of his morning-after (how it all comes back) and workless for once until evening, all keen to come shopping with me, even to wait while I have my hair done, something Robert would never consider, or to meet me somewhere afterwards. But I can't face this, much as I appreciate it : there is so little time left to be alone in my flat and my city. So we have a shower and make love again and brew fresh coffee, and I finally get him to drop me at Alexis', who is screaming by now, because I am late, but really late, not just the amount he always allows me. I hate Alexis being angry with me – the Slav sulk that follows the screams is quite something – and I dread the possibility of technical reprisals on my hair so I have to say : 'Alexis, *Tony* suddenly turned up, after all this time,' and immediately it's all right, as I knew it would be, and he says, 'Oh, I see. You want Elastoplast?' and we laugh and he tells me all the latest scandal and my hair comes out beautifully, an Alexis-special, and I love Alexis and wish, just for a moment, that he wasn't one hundred per cent queer, because it would be so cosy, especially with our two names.

It's a lovely afternoon by now and I take myself out to lunch and enjoy the lovely solitary anonymity of eating alone in London. I sit at a pavement table for coffee, showing off my legs and writing little notes to all my suitable friends suggesting they phone Christine at my flat and take her out for dinners and parties and drinks. I see a lovely man at the next table but he's much too absorbed in a rather plain girl so we just give each other the occasional long look from behind our dark glasses. It's much warmer today, it's going to be spring, maybe summer, and I stroll up the road looking at the shops and longing to go in and buy something unnecessary. But I can't, somehow; I feel time running out and a terrible melancholy beginning to spread over me. So I go for a walk by the river instead, but that's also a mistake for it looks so dirty and beautiful with the sun on it that it makes me want to cry and I wonder why I have never lived on a houseboat – and shall I one day or is it already too late? I go home, abruptly, in a panic that I shall not be able to force myself to leave London at all, and I phone my agent who makes encouraging noises about possible film sales which I never believe till the cheque arrives. I pack, in an angry, messy rush, having discovered the train that I ought to catch, and walk round the flat feeling so sentimental that I think, Christ, any minute I am going to start talking to it and how maudlin can you get? I catch myself thinking goodbye little flat and I rush out in a violent hurry, the way you leave a man you want to stay with, and hail a convenient cab. It nearly chokes me to say Liverpool Street and as we drive along I actually start to cry, but seriously, not the kind of tears you can choose whether or not to shed, and I ruin my eyes so thank God for dark glasses again. We just hit the rush hour and I start to pray I shall miss the train (my mother and I actually do believe quite firmly in God, though a deity made very much to our own specifications) but I don't because the wretched, well-meaning driver makes it a point of honour to be clever and get me there just in time and I have to tip him for *that*. He'll never know how much more he'd have got for being late. I fall into the train, cursing, just as it moves, and I've exhausted my tears by now, but my face is quite ruined so

I keep on my glasses and sit there in my corner, as we move out, closing my eyes so as not to see what I am leaving behind.

## *18*

CHRISTINE has left a list of instructions. (A day in the life of a busy mother.) I asked her to do this, and in detail, knowing the full extent of my own ignorance, but I must admit surprise. It reads like a fatigue roster from Reveille to the Last Post. She watches me read it and I think she looks both guilty and amused.

'Oh well,' I say. 'Maybe it looks worse on paper, like recipes and knitting patterns.' (Not that I have ever actually read a knitting pattern.)

She smiles. 'Well.' Had I not been personally involved I would have rejoiced to see a look of such cynicism on her face. 'I've put asterisks against all the really important things. You can let the house get as dirty as you like. It's just the kids, really. Don't worry, they won't let you neglect them. They'll yell.'

I say dubiously, 'Oh good,' and look again at the list. 'What a lot of little asterisks.'

'Yes. I'm afraid so. They're hungry little monsters. And – oh, I am so sorry about the nappies.'

'Don't be. It's time I learnt the facts of life.' Privately I wonder why I, who can deal quite happily with cat-shit and dog-shit, should retch without fail at human excrement. I look forward resignedly to a lot of retching.

Christine suddenly hugs me, saying passionately, 'Oh, you *are* an angel.'

'Go quickly,' I say .'Before I change my mind.'

'Let Paul do everything the minute he gets in,' she says. 'It will do him good. And his mother will come in over the week-end.' She's flushed and starry. 'Oh, I can't believe it. London. I'm actually going. I'll take the greatest care of your flat.'

'Oh, that's all right,' I say. 'Just answer the 'phone. I've told all kinds of people to ring you up.'

'Golly,' she says, taking me back years. I nearly panic : I want to grab her and say, Let's both go. Or let's forget the whole thing. I can't, now it comes to the point, make myself believe that I – *I* – am actually going to spend another week here with two children and no Christine. And Paul. I nearly say, Don't go. I am not responsible. Do you realize what you may be doing leaving me here? I want her to shoulder the blame well in advance, before there is any to shoulder.

'You just have a good time,' I say, 'and don't worry about a thing.'

*Day* 1. Departure 1300 hours. Cries of Mummy, howls and screams.

Bribery campaign at once, quite shameless. Sweets galore and orange drinks and Ribena and yes, of course you can make mud pies in the garden, I rocking baby the while. God, it smells. Already? Oh, not already. God? Please, God? Yes, already. Hold breath and half-close eyes. Into pail with magic stuff in it. Wipe. Oh, God. Ugh. This can't be me doing this. Clean one. Fold as taught. So far so good. Apply ointments and powder, for we mustn't get a rash now, must we? (Why not?) Now then. If only it would keep still. Amazing how they *squirm*. I shall castrate it, or circumcise it at least, with this pin if it doesn't stop moving. Ah, got it. How long can the mud pies suffice? An ominous silence from the garden. No matter. Onward, to plastic pants. Of all revolting garments. They must be somewhere. I only just took them off. Yells. Yells from outside. Window. Oh, my God. Well, if you will have a stream at the bottom of your garden what can you expect? '*Michael.*' No. '*Simon.*' (Which one is it?) Dump baby on floor, where it can fear no fall at least. Dash. Muddy, dripping two-year-old, bawling with terror. Stream only few inches deep but still, it could have held its face under out of sheer perversity. (Look at it this way, Christine, a short life and a gay one. Only half the work. Good excuse for the next one.) Oh well. Soothing noises. What fun. What an adventure. And don't you ever do that again or I'll *kill* you. Own clothes totally ruined. Never liked this dress very much and I suppose it will clean. Comfort, comfort. There, there. Aren't we all wet and silly? Look! Isn't it fun? Idiotic. How do you talk to them when you can't understand what they say? And how patiently they repeat the identical gibberish for you, meeting with the identical incomprehension. No wonder they get frustrated. Return. Now we all need a wash and a change, don't we, and – God, where's it gone? I left it right there. Simon, where's Michael? (Take his mind off his own troubles.) Or maybe Michael, where's Simon? (Must get this sorted out.) No help. No interest at all. Self-centred from the word go. No wonder adults are selfish. But it can't have got far, it's only a year ... Crawled off somewhere, bugger it – ah, there you are, behind the – my God, what's that in your *mouth?* It's only trying to poison itself, just to spite me. Ignore howls of drowned one, prise open its jaws. Ugh, God. Sticky, wet . . . and *black*. What the hell is it? Christ, coal. It's eating coal. Come on, give. Like dog. Wish it were. Fish out the bits. Throw away. Wipe. And still no plastic pants to be seen. Maybe it ate those first.

\*     \*     \*

'They've gone down remarkably well.'

'Yes, thank God.'

'What ever did you do?'

'Wore them out.'

'Are you sure it wasn't the other way round?'

'Oh, I'm sure it was both. Do I look as beat as I feel?' (God forbid.)

'No. You look wonderful.'

Pause.

'Well, I suppose I better get on with some marking.'

'Yes. I suppose I better make tracks for the typewriter.'

'How's it going?'

'Oh, it's not. But it will. It must.'

Pause.

'Alexa.'

'Yes, Paul?'

'This is ... all very good of you.'
'Don't be silly.'

\*         \*         \*

*Well, I don't know how to put it, see, it's sort of private
and special, you know, and it doesn't matter if it's not like
as exciting as it used to be 'cos that's not it, it's kind of something else. Like if you go to church, like at Xmas or Easter,
and you take communion, you know, well, you feel kind of
new again, don't you, and it sort of strengthens you, I don't
know, I can't really explain what I mean. But it's like that,
sort of.'*

Damn, the shift key is playing up again.

\*         \*         \*

So here we all lie in our separate beds. You, Paul, in the
next room in your double-bed, all alone. Me here in my
single, a bleary-eyed typist with cream on her face. And
you, Christine, in my big bed where I slept with Tony last
night, but I changed the sheets for you, though you needn't
worry in any case. Tony's the cleanest person I know, it
goes with his fetish for blood. How do you feel – is it funny
not being together? Never apart, you told me (proudly,
regretfully?) except for the times in hospital. So now, how
do you like it? You're there in my flat, with my things
around you; does the traffic keep you awake? I have your
silence all to myself now. Your children are asleep. Do you
miss them? Or are you out in the streets breathing dirty night
air and petrol fumes, walking and looking, revisiting all
your past haunts and feeling old? You could be anywhere :
we only know what you told us. So what, after all, is real?
Only what we know.

(But we didn't, Christine. Not that first night. Not a word,
not a touch. Only looked.)
Be happy, Christine. Enjoy yourself. Make the most of
it. That's all I'm here for, in fact. I just want you to be
happy.

\*         \*         \*

*Day* 2. The long trek to the shops. Even twenty-four hours make certain priorities clear. Two all-enveloping nylon overalls for me, and millions of disposable nappies. I don't care if they're bad for their bottoms, they're good for my morale. Let them worry about their own bottoms. I'll have the same neat washed pile when Christine gets back that she left me before she went, and all credit to me. So they maybe get a little rash, but only maybe. I can always pile on more of that ghastly soothing cream. To think of that being massaged into *my* bottom twenty-five years ago: sounds like a brand new perversion. Anyway, who knows, why should they be allergic? Maybe they'll love disposable nappies. I certainly will. It may not be an ethical point in any case; Christine probably can't afford them. Perhaps I should lay in a stock for her.

All these people here, shopping day in, day out? Do they read my books? Am I in the local library? Will they see the magazine feature? Well, it's not over yet, maybe I should grab one or two and squeeze in the odd extra interview. 'Excuse me, I'm . . .' No, perhaps not.

Simple food, protein and salad and cereal. No time for any-thing elaborate with all the washing – changing and feeding and following round. Don't let them out of your sight for a second, that's the obvious motto, after yesterday's little escapade. But bottles of wine, to see me through, and cigar-ettes, as for a siege. Pile up the pram. Who knows when I'll get out again. Like *Girl of the Limberlost* or something equally corny.

At least one of them can be pinned down, more or less. Pram or play-pen, makes no odds. But the other one, oh boy. The games. That indescribable chattering probably means 'I'm bored, amuse me, what shall I do now?' Oddly rewarding when you get a smile, a laugh; better still ten minutes of peace. Time to read Robert's letter. Oh God, another one. Yes, my love, yes, we would do all that and more, and again and again till we died of it if we were lucky, if you were with me, if I were with you. And Lucas

is going over big, is she, now does that mean professionally?
I don't care, I don't, it's your life, and it means damn all, it
means Tony, no more. And why don't I join you, meet your
mother, your father? Yes, indeed, why don't I, but when?
You don't envisage (lovely old-fashioned word, how Ameri-
cans mingle the old and the new) getting back in the near
future. Oh.

*       *       *

Bricks, water, sand, toys with wheels. Books for staring at
and then hurling into space to see how far you can throw.
It's all so tactile, I know how you feel. At two you could
start your own little psychedelic movement. Let's have a
happening. Oh, we have. Not quite what I had in mind.
Great distress, because we only have nappies at night now,
don't we? We are a big boy now, aren't we? We are *clean*.
Never mind, it was all that concentration on the game. I
know. Hard to think of two things at once, and some of us
never learn. Okay, so we change them, so what's one pair
of pants between friends? Don't cry like that, kid. We all
disgrace ourselves from time to time, I should know. You
catch me next time I'm drunk, that'll show you, and please
God make it soon. I'm surprised mothers aren't permanently
sloshed. Oh well, having got this far, why not? Open bottle.
Maybe we should all have some. A lovely somnolent torpor
is what we all need, perfect peace to greet Paul, the returning
breadwinner, schoolmaster, husband and father ... Christ,
how does Christine stand it? Okay, quiet spell on knee.
Amazingly heavy. Large glass of wine, small nursery
rhymes. Over the disgrace now, the unmentionable. Only
don't kid yourself it won't happen again. You shouldn't
have such high standards, child, you'll only make yourself
unhappy. I'm quite popular. No, don't exaggerate. I'm
acceptable. I've been here long enough to be part of the
scene. I'm Lexa. Why is it nice to be smiled at? We've
nothing in common. But at least you know they're not
pretending and if they want to be beastly they will, and out
in the open.

Yes, well, that didn't last long. Now for the violent bit. We

hurl cushions at each other, wildly and laboriously. Sometimes our aim's not too good but of course there's not much
breakable stuff left so that's all right. We take careful aim
at each other and miss. It takes a lot of effort. Wakes other
one. Howls. It does cry a lot. More than it should? Who
knows? Other one goes to investigate, comfort. Comfort?
Yes, this time, but you never can tell; yesterday he went
over lovingly and poked it in eye, with deafening results.

Check, no, dry for once, thank God, and can't be hungry:
the amount it consumes by clock and demand. Christine
will return to a case of gross obesity. Can a one-year-old get
obese in a week? Well, if anyone can, this one can. But food
is so soothing and don't we all know it. So it must want
picking up. Love. How do you administer love automatically? If I were its mother would I love it, just like that?
Presumably not, else no need of N.S.P.C.C. But probably.
Oh well. Pick up and cuddle, regardless. Rock to and fro.
Maybe it won't notice the difference. It's not so bad really
and I suppose it will look more human later on when it gets
some more hair. All right, enough. Enough? Yes. Okay,
kid, crawl. Crawl to your heart's content and see if I care. It
can certainly shift, though; amazing. That curious crab-like
motion. Standing up efforts are brave, and the few stagger-
ing steps, but generally lead to collapse in a matter of
seconds. Now they're both at it, walking and crawling,
climbing all over each other. How funny to think they will
grow into *men*.

\*     \*     \*

'I think you're coping marvellously.'
'Oh, come. Let's not exaggerate. I'm surviving. You're
doing your own shirts and the house is in chaos and the
meals are lamentable. But apart from that.'
'The kids seem happy enough.'
'Oh, they're washed and fed and put to bed. That's
survival.'
'No, I think you do a little more than that.'
'Oh well. I pull the odd funny face.'
    Huge yawn.

'Are you worn out?'

'No. Yes.'

'Poor Alexa.'

'It's all right. It's good for me. Good healthy exhaustion. Nice and physical for a change, not like bashing my brains out on that machine.' Would that I were, though; I'm way behind.

'Yes, I'm worried about your work. Is all this ... nonsense interfering with it terribly?'

'Doesn't matter. I've still got time. And I work better under pressure.' But *this* kind of pressure?

\*     \*     \*

'Mother'll be here tomorrow.'

'Oh, yes?'

'Mm. I'll be able to take you out for a break. If you'd like that. She can't stay the night, of course, there's no room, but she promised to come and help out for the afternoons and evenings over the weekend.'

'Bliss.'

'You're really pleased?'

'Yes, of course. My God, another pair of hands.'

'Mm. I think – sometimes I think Chris rather resents her.'

Steady now. 'Oh well, that's quite different, isn't it?'

Deadlock.

\*     \*     \*

But we sit on. Presumably he ought to be marking. I certainly ought to be typing. But I can't move; I'm whacked. No wonder Christine doesn't open the piano lid much. 'Television?'

'Lovely. About all I'm fit for.' Casual cosy smile, but I watch the lines of his body through his clothes as he moves across the room to switch on the set. Not significant, of course, because I always do it, to Alexis in the salon, to men working on building sites. But oh, lovely lines of shoulders and back under the shirt, lovely low-slung belt on narrow hips with narrow trousers to match on nice long legs. Very presentable. This won't do at all. I only had Tony the day before yesterday, well yesterday, if you count the repeat, and Tony was meant to be, among other things, my insurance policy. Though whatever made me think I could stoke up like that I can't imagine. It's never worked before. I'm not a hibernating animal.

They can't get BBC 2 so our intellectual pretensions are not put to the test. We watch a spy thing (they're unavoidable really) and laugh at it to show our superiority. All very domestic and comfortable. But why does he have such a strong personality when he's really so nondescript?

'Have some wine.'

'Oh, is there any? I thought we'd run out.'

'I got some more.' Guilty laugh. 'To see me through the children.' Another few days and I'll be taking drugs.

'You're spoiling me.'

We drink. We watch. Now what do I expect the wine to do? Put me to sleep? I wonder.

'This is great.' Relaxes. Stretches out. Lovely tight trousers. 'This is the life. You should come more often.'

'Yes.' I should.

'Suppose these people make a packet out of this kind of thing.' Waves hand at screen.

'Yes.'

'Amazing.' Sighs. 'Oh well, I'm probably just jealous.'

\*        \*        \*

Is this what it's like, marriage? Do he and Christine sit here night after night watching this kind of thing and exchanging odd, disconnected remarks? Would it be like this for me if I married someone? My parents did it, of course, but about twice a week when they were both in together and not entertaining. But mostly they talked or played cards. There was often music, and a lot of laughter. Can't decide if that sounds demented or Victorian.

'I'll make some coffee.' He looks grateful. I go out, into Christine's kitchen. I just about know where everything is now but it still feels strange among another woman's things. Absurd that kitchens are so personal. Wrong somehow. Comment on our materialistic society and the Woman's Role.

Starting point for protest article, perhaps? No, overdone, and I've got enough on already. Leave the *Guardian* to Erin.

'Oh, Paul.' Shock.

'I came to give you a hand.'

'That's all right, I can manage. You'll miss the end.'

'Oh, it's over. The goodies survived and the baddies shot each other in a mad fit of treachery.'

'Really? How very surprising. What a high moral tone we get for our licence fee. Most uplifting.'

We are beginning to talk alike. Alarm.

'Alexa.'

'It's nearly ready. You go back. I'll bring it in.' My knees are shaking. This is ridiculous.

I go out with the tray and promptly bump into him, hovering in the passage. He touches me.

'Don't. I'll drop everything.'

'I'll take it.'

I hang on : absurd tug of war. We look at each other. I let go. He takes the tray out of my hands and puts it on the hallstand amongst gloves and mackintoshes. It's hopeless. He touches me again. I can't say anything; what is there to say? Unhand me, sir. I'm not that kind of girl. (Aren't I?) Your wife is my friend. Impossible. We kiss. Gently at first, tasting, then madly, devouring each other. Like school dances. Crazy. Back to my youth. I get all the old authentic rubbish, blood pounding, knees to jelly, heart and stomach revolving. Delightful. His hands all over me. I want him.

We stop.

'God, you're beautiful.'

'Look, Paul, don't turn me on. Only I don't turn off easily.'

'Then don't. Don't turn off. Christ, can't you *feel* how I want you?' He presses against me, lovely and hard, all ready for me. Irresistible.

'Yes, I can feel.' We kiss for punctuation, but differently again, licking each other indulgently.

'Don't you want me at all?'

Anger. 'Oh yes, yes. God, what d'you think, can't you tell? Don't be so bloody-minded. D'you want me to spell it out for you?' Yes, I want you. Yes, I want to make love. Yes, I want to go to bed with you. Yes, I want you to fuck me. All right, will that do?' Then I pull back a little, for my last-ditch stand. His eyes are extraordinary. I never knew blue could be such a hot colour. 'But not, not, *not* if you're going to feel guilty about it. Because that's death.'

He swallows. He gathers me up again, folding me into him. How well our bodies fit. The grand old illusion, every time. And all the clichés in the book. This can't be wrong because it feels so right. Etcetera, etcetera. Ad nauseam in excelsis. 'I won't if you won't. Promise.'

For a moment I think we are going to do it right there in the hall, standing up against the wall or lying down on the narrow strip of carpet. Then he starts pulling me with him, entwined, back to the sitting-room, kissing all the time, murmuring each other's names.

'Promise.'

Upstairs a child cries. We freeze.

\*       \*       \*

While he's gone, I make it easy for him. Can't remember when last I had such a bad moment though; not for years and years. I write him a note, hand shaking, writing all over the place. (A valuable addition to the Collected Correspondence of Alexa King in some American University years hence?) 'I'm going to bed. Expect you will think better of it. No hard feelings. See you at breakfast. A.' Now I can't do more than that. Short of walking out into the night like Oates to defend my – what? I drop the note on the floor where he can't miss it and creep up the stairs, into my room (luckily the nearest) and press the door shut. He's in the nursery, soothing. Even hearing his voice makes me tremble. I'm in such a state. I sit on the bed and touch myself hesitantly but it's not what I want, not enough. I want so much more. And – am still hoping somewhere secretly behind my own back? No. *No*. Why so vehement? 'Methinks the lady doth protest too much.' Cigarette, the great standby. Swig from a bottle of my hidden cache of whisky. Oh, God,

pathetic. Look at my face in the mirror, written all over it.
Is there anything more absurd than disappointed lust? Put
out the light. Better in the dark. Cool, soothing darkness. It
will pass, it will pass. Getting better, already. Yes I *am*.
There now, nothing much, just a mad little incident doomed
to oblivion. Poor Paul. Hope he doesn't feel too bad. That
time on the beach rocked him quite enough. But I really
never expected ... didn't I?

Think of that tray of coffee, cooling itself on the hall-stand.

The main trouble is, I can't see what harm it would do.
Might do good. Oh, Mother, you ruined my moral values.
Or set me free.

Two more cigarettes. Half an hour maybe. Some more
whisky. Cool blood again in the dark and the quiet. Peace.
All the same really, now, whether we did or we didn't, which
makes it so pointless. Non-existent. Just an experience
missed. That's my trouble : I try to cram in too much.
'Excuse me, sir, but you look rather nice and I do have an
hour to spare.' Hardly. But almost.

Near to sleep, footsteps, dreaming or real? A creak on the
stairs. But I was somewhere else, there were people, I think
... voices. Have I been asleep? Then doorhandle. Real.
    'Alexa. I can't. Will you? Can we? I— oh, Alexa.'
Stumbling, incoherent, pleading, desperate. And my hunger
all gone. So I hold out my arms in friendship and pity with
no hesitation.

*        *        *

    'I'm sorry.'
    'Hush. That word is forbidden.' Stroking him, stroking
him.
    'Much too quick. Oh, God ...'
    'Ssh.' Kiss to silence him. He's quite right, of course,
much too quick, and too clumsy, unco-ordinated, emotional,
badly-timed, all these things, but who cares? There are
other things, too. Instead of skill, need. Kiss and stroke.

116

'I didn't mean it to be like that.'

'I know. It's all right.'

'Is it, really? Are you all right?' Such a terribly anxious voice. He seems as young as his children.

'Of course I'm all right.'

'Really?' Hope, wanting to believe me.

'Really. You could tell if I wasn't. I'd be twitching.' Of course I didn't come, but who cares for once? I was so far from coming it was quite something else and in its way lovely. Who wants the same thing every time? Funny, though. After that high-powered beginning. A nice touch of irony.

'You see ... it's been so long.' Yes, I could tell. And how he cried out. That's a gift in itself. 'You see, Chris and I ...' Ah, good, he can mention her name. That's one hurdle over. 'Oh, I don't know, maybe I shouldn't tell you ...' Hung up.

'Cigarette?'

'Thanks.' He gropes in the dark, not ready yet for the light. Oh well, he can't help it. Passes me one. That's better.

'Talk if you like. Tell me. Or don't. It's all right either way.' People are only people, with troubles, and meant to comfort each other in bed.

Smokes a bit. 'Oh, I don't know. I don't mean there's anything wrong, it's just ... Since the baby ... all sort of meaningless for her, and this contraceptive business, she doesn't—' Thought. 'Hell, and I never even asked you, my God—' Tense.

'I'm okay. It's all right.' Feel him relax.

'Well, she just doesn't like it, never has. I don't know what it is, we've tried everything.'

'I know.'

'Has she talked to you about it?'

'A bit.'

'Well, do *you* understand? Maybe another woman ... God.' Reflects .'How circular it all is.'

'She seems to have a big maternal thing going, I think. She—' Careful, not to betray. 'I think complete safety disturbs her.'

'God. Yes, I thought so. I thought that was it, or part of

it. But God, on my salary. And I keep thinking, if only we get a breathing space now, we can get on our feet a bit, maybe even pay someone ... she'd have time for her music again.'

'Yes, I know. But that's looking ahead. I don't know if Christine can do that.' How much can I say? 'And I think in a way that you and the children have replaced it.'

'Have we? Maybe we have. But she's not happy, is she? You can see she's not happy.' (Are you?) 'Oh, she's been better lately, but before you came – oh, it's been deathly.' Pause. 'God, what a word to pick. It's been *nothing*.'

Try. Nothing venture, etcetera. 'Do you think maybe that's it?'

'What?'

'Well, an absence of something. Maybe drama. Whereas risking a baby, being pregnant, having it. Even losing it ...' Funny, I hadn't even considered it consciously and now it all comes. Like the old joke. "How do I know what I think till I hear what I say?" ... 'Maybe it gives her—'

'What?' Suddenly bitter. 'Something to live for?'

'Well, a sort of focal point.'

Pause, while this sinks in. Have I said too much? I only want to help. Truthfully. As God is my witness. Where are you, God? Go on, inspire me.

'But I—' Stops. Yes, I know, you should be her focal point, you mean. Is she yours? Unfair question. You have more in your life. Never mind. Changes tack. 'Damn it all, we've got two kids already. Oh, don't get me wrong, they're terrific, but they do wear her out.'

'Yes, I know. But it isn't a rational thing. You can't expect it to be.'

Sighs, defeated. 'Is it ... a feminine thing, do you think?'

Oh dear, over the border into the no-man's land of sex warfare. Feminine. For feminine read illogical. Or to be polite, intuitive, emotional. 'I don't know. Maybe. That, and ... just Christine herself. I don't know.' Pounces. 'Well, would you be like that? Can you imagine feeling like that?' Juggling with honesty, tact, genuine doubt. 'I'm not sure. I don't think so. But we're not all that alike. We just have certain things in common. But I've got my work and that

... makes a difference.' How hard the words are to choose. I've noticed before, I never talk as well as I write. What flows on the page comes haltingly from the tongue. Just as well, or a pity? Who knows? 'Maybe Christine's more typical than I am.' And I try to think. But I don't know anyone I would call typical of anything.

'Maybe. That's the trouble.'

'What is?'

'Oh, we married so young, Chris and I. Well, comparatively. And we ... went out together for years beforehand. Of course, we went out with other people, too, but ... nothing too serious.'

Is he trying to tell me he's never had anyone else? Does he mind? 'Yes, well, that happens a lot nowadays. Lots of students I knew—'

'Yes, sure, it's fine. Only now – well, I don't really know what I'm up against. I've no real standard—' He wants to say comparison. He can't. It sticks in his throat. It smacks of disloyalty. And here he is, still in my bed. 'Paul, I don't think a dozen steady girl-friends way back in the past would help you now. Maybe half a dozen marriages would. Maybe not.'

I wanted to give him a joke, however slight, to lighten the gloom. He ignores it. Did I speak in bad taste or just cut across his track? 'Mm. The thing is— God knows, I've tried not to admit this—' (Is he going to say it?) '—even to myself—' (He has.) '—but I just don't understand Chris. Does that make sense? Can you love someone without understanding them?'

'Yes.' How little he knows. Poor Paul. 'I think so. Very easily.'

'Because . . . I really do love Chris. You know? Do you believe that?'

He means do I think he's a swine. Oh God, why must people be like this? Every married man I've ever known, when he's not tearing her up is telling you how much he loves her, just to make sure. Why shouldn't you love her? I want you to love her. Good God, why shouldn't I? 'Of course I believe that. It's obvious.'

'Even . . .' He can't.

'Oh, Paul, of course. Don't be silly. If I didn't I wouldn't be here. Because *that* could be dangerous.'

Turns to me. Kisses me. 'God, I'm glad you are.'

'What, dangerous?' Can't resist it.

'No, here.' Kiss. 'I've been such a bastard to you.'

'Well.' Teasing.

'Yes, I have. I know I have. I've watched myself. Just sheer bloody-mindedness and envy.' Kiss. Starting again. Rising up, growing, turning me on. 'So much that I wanted and couldn't have. Taking it out on you because I thought ...'

It's much better this time. Much slower and longer and surprisingly calculated. Luxurious. He's quite different. That's what I like, finding out. Giving no help or not much, fitting in, going along. God, he's good. How extraordinary. No words, a heavy-breathing silence, heat and heartbeats and the bedclothes on the floor. And I come for him and I cry out his name.

# 19

'Paul tells me you're managing very well.'

'Oh. Well, that's very kind of him, Mrs Davies, but really I'm just muddling through.'

'Mm ...?' Vague. Wistful, even. Am I managing too well perhaps? 'The children certainly seem to have taken to you.'

'Oh, they've got used to me, luckily.' Modest, unassuming. Just the right tone – I hope.

'I think it's more than that. Michael's been telling me about all the exciting things he's been doing with Auntie Alexa.' Bright pink and white smile; Paul's sharp blue eyes vivid in pale, lined face. Jealous as hell. And inaccurate. Michael calls me Lexa; I soon cured him of all that Auntie rubbish.

'Oh, has he? I play the odd game with him, that's all.'

And bribe him into peace when I fail to exhaust him. Has he told you about all the illicit sweets and ice-cream and lollies?

'Mm.' How funny, she says it just like Paul. Wish his father was alive, I like to reassemble people from their parents. 'How's Christine, have you heard from her?'

'Paul had a phone call, just to say she'd arrived safely. That's all.'

'Well, I do hope she's enjoying herself. She deserves a rest, she works so hard. Don't you think so?'

'I certainly do.'

'She'll miss the children though. And Paul, of course.'

'Of course.'

Sigh. Stacking plates. 'I do hope she won't be lonely. London is such a big place to be on your own.'

The old myth. So's Essex. So's anywhere. 'Oh well, it's only for a week.'

'Yes.' Pause. 'It's really very kind of you, Alexa, to give up so much of your time when you're so busy.'

How odd she makes my name sound. Does she actually hate me or merely resent me or is it just that she finds me puzzling? 'It's nothing, I'm enjoying it.'

'Ah.' Deliberate misinterpretation of my social politeness. 'Ah well, I expect you'll have children of your own one day.'

Only one way to handle that : don't be drawn. 'It's quite possible.' Patronising old bitch, wants to believe kids are the height of every woman's ambition or ought to be.

'So that's something to look forward to.' My life so empty – she hopes? Mustn't laugh. Rude. 'You must be very lonely at times, living all by yourself in London.'

'Well. Not really. I'm awfully busy, most of the time. And I do know quite a lot of people who tend to drop in and stay.' Well, why not? Don't tempt me, lady, that's all.

'Oh.' Digests this. 'Your mother . . . she's on television, isn't she?'

'Yes. Alexandra Fortune. Panel games and rubbish like that.' She'll think that sounds disrespectful. Fun.

'Oh. I believe I've seen her then. She's ... a remarkable personality.'

Funny – she's got it exactly right for once. 'Yes.'

'And your father?'

'Dead.' Even now it hurts to say that.

'Oh dear.' Embarrassed. 'I *am* sorry. Was it – long ago?'

'Years. And it seems like yesterday.' God, I've said something real to her at last. She doesn't know how to take it. Moves on.

'So your poor mother's all alone. I *do* feel for her, I know what that's like only too well. She must be very lonely.'

'Well.' Not exactly. Although yes, in a way. Fall back on cliché .'She has a very active social life.'

'Oh.' Can hear her pondering what this may mean. 'Oh, good. And you must be a great comfort to her. But I expect she's looking forward to grandchildren.' Heavy hint? Get married and do your duty : get out of my son's life.

'Well, not really. She's got two already and she rather thinks that's enough.'

'Oh.'

'My brother has a wife.'

'I didn't know you had a brother. Good gracious. Your mother doesn't look old enough to be a grandmother.' Envy? Or reproof?

'No. She's very glamorous, isn't she?' Oh, lovely mother. I only hope you are half as proud of me. 'Well, she married at eighteen, which helped.'

'Did she? Good heavens.' Very genteel. 'Was ... your father in television, too?'

'No. Newspapers. He was Alexander King.' And I only just stopped myself saying, in an excess of filial pride, THE Alexander King.

'Was he?' Impressed. 'He was very famous then, wasn't he?'

'Yes.' Smug.

'That must be where you get it from.'

'What?' As if I didn't know.

'Your writing.'

Oh yes, yes. My writing. 'Well, he was an editor as well as a journalist. It's not quite the same thing.' And at one time in our house there were four people answering to Alex, till Peter Alexander rebelled.

'I see.' She doesn't. 'Still, it must be part of it.'

'Oh yes, undoubtedly.' And you should see my mother's letters. No, you shouldn't.

'Well. Shall we make a cup of tea?'

'Oh yes. Do let's.' My, aren't we polite. On with the kettle.

'Paul should be back soon.' Is she searching my face? God, does she *know*? Is there a ghastly maternal intuition at work?

'Yes.' Paul and Michael at some old school function, Simon peacefully asleep. Not the kind of afternoon she expected. Only me to probe.

'He works so hard.'

'Yes.' Don't we all?

'I'm so glad he's got such a nice steady girl as Christine. She's such a good wife and mother. I was quite worried when he first went up to the University. As well as being proud of him, I mean. Students are such a mixed bunch these days, aren't they? He could have met anyone. That's why it was such a relief when he came home with Christine.'

'Yes.' What *am* I supposed to say?

'She's such a *nice* girl. Whereas some of them are quite wild, aren't they, and ... well, messy. Art students for example. All that long hair and strange clothing.'

'Christine used to have long hair.'

'Did she? Oh, perhaps she did. But she was never ... well, you know what I mean. Oh, I suppose all mothers worry too much, we can't help it, but I was always afraid Paul might marry someone a bit too ... wild, you know, selfish, too set on having a career, that kind of thing. Someone who wouldn't make a proper home for him. But Christine has been absolutely splendid. They really are an ideal couple. And it's so good for the children to grow up in a musical home.'

I really cannot stand much more of this. Christine, my love, they are trying to destroy you, even your past. Oh, make the most of your week of freedom; this old cow will probably make sure you never get another.

'Yes. I think my mother worried a bit. But she's absolutely enchanted with Catherine – my brother's wife. She's a model.'

'Oh.' Instant shock instantly veiled. Succeeded by blank amazement. 'But I thought you said they had two small children.'

'Yes. I did.'

'Oh. Then you mean she used to be a model.'

'No. She still is. In fact her career is going better than ever. When she was pregnant she modelled a lot of maternity wear and she was thin again just in time for short skirts and long hair. She's lucky, she's just the right type for the current fashions.' Oh Catherine, I wish you were here. Not that you'd help me be rude, you wouldn't open your beautiful mouth, you never do, but at least I could show you off.

'Good heavens. How on earth does she manage all that with two small children?'

'Simple. She has a nanny.'

'Really.' Pause. 'But even so, well, however good they are, these people, they must need a lot of supervision.'

'Not at all. Not this one anyway, she fits in beautifully. Catherine's off to Paris soon on a modelling job without a care in the world.' I hope that's true. Anyway, it's effective.

'And your brother doesn't mind? I do think young people are extraordinary. Flitting around the world leaving a husband and two small children at home. I expect you'll think me old-fashioned but I just can't see how that kind of thing can be good for a marriage.'

'Peter's very proud of her.' Defiantly. 'And so is my mother. We all are. Even the children. They love all the clothes. They look at pictures of Catherine and say "Pretty Mummy".'

God knows where it all might have ended but the kettle saves us : it boils and clicks and we start making tea. Into this charming cameo of domestic harmony steps Paul returning with Michael and mingled cries of 'Granny' and 'Lexa'. We have a Christine-type nursery tea, which I have carefully prepared to show what I can do, (God, why does one bother to compete?) but I only exchange one type of discomfort for another : Mrs Davies' eyes flit constantly from Paul to me. My face is blank, I know; I don't have to see it; after so much practice the shutter comes down automatically. But Paul ... oh love, you're no good at it, are you? You don't know how. The way you look at me ... If I were the onlooker and we were another couple, I should *know*. But perhaps my blank face will put Mrs Davies off. Perhaps she will only think – quite bad enough – that you fancy me.

The baby wakes and cries; I spring up – a merciful release. Mrs Davies murmurs offers of help above Michael's incoherent recital of his day's events. 'Not at all, thank you. I can manage.' And I take as long as I can.

## 20

'GOD, I thought she'd never go. Why the hell did you ask her to stay?'

'Well, I only said if she liked she could have my bed and I'd sleep on the couch. I thought it was only polite.'

'Another time let me worry about being polite to my own blasted mother.'

He's really angry. Amazing. 'If she'd stayed much later she'd have missed the last bus and I'd have had to run her home.'

'Yes, well, that might not have been a bad thing.'

'What do you mean? God, can't you see how much I want to be alone with you?'

I get up. My turn to be angry. 'Yes, and so can she. If she's got half a brain in her head she'll have guessed. I never thought I should warn you, I thought it was obvious, we'd both be dead careful. But you – the way you looked at me. And you hardly talked to her you were so busy lighting my fags.' Which reminds me, and I light one now. 'That's why I haven't had one for the last hour. I had to do something to stop you. You even let her put the kids to bed so you could stay down here with me.'

'Well, what's wrong with that? She enjoys it.'

'Yes, but you don't usually do it. That's what's wrong with it. Christ! Do I have to spell it out for you?'

'Is that why you rushed in the garden?'

'Yes. Good God, yes. So she could see me from the window and know we weren't – petting in the parlour or whatever.' I pause for breath, fuming. I am using up my cigarette so fast I am nearly choking myself. 'And you usually run her home, don't you?'

'Well ... quite often. Not always.'

'No. But tonight you didn't. Of all the nights to pick. Well, now do you see?'

His face is what used to be called a study. All my anger dissolves in a wave of pity and warmth. Poor human being, unused to dissembling, unmasked, accused. Poor love, you make me feel old.

'Was it really as bad as that?' Humble.

'Oh, I don't know.' I want to reassure him now. What else can I do? 'I just think we should be very careful and distant. No. More sort of jolly, like brother and sister. And talk about Christine a bit more. You never even mentioned her name.'

Guilty but genuine surprise. 'Didn't I?'

'No. You're supposed to be missing her, you know. But when your mother mentioned her you just looked extremely furtive and said nothing.'

'Oh, God.' Breaks up, to my relief, into young, shame-faced smile. 'I'm no good at this at all, am I?'

I have to laugh, and he holds out his arms for me. 'Well. Let's say you could do with a little more practice.' I put my face against his chest and kiss him through his shirt. Lovely warm clean body-smell.

'Mm. I certainly could.' Kisses the top of my head. 'Let's hope I get it. God, your hair's fantastic.' Digs both hands into it on either side of my head and gathers up fistfuls, making me look at him. 'And your eyes. Extraordinary. You're like a lion.'

'Well.'

'All right, lioness. But you really are. You're – everything my mother ever tried to save me from.'

'What do you mean?'

'Oh – life. Excitement. Danger. The wrong kind of girl.'

'Yes. I rather gathered that. In fact that's another thing

I must mention. I more or less got the big warning-off speech this afternoon when you were out with Michael.'

I feel him stiffen. 'What?'

'All about your happy marriage and Christine's manifold virtues. All of which I agree with. But very nastily presented. Loaded, you might say. Full of innuendo about children and career girls.'

'Oh, God.' He strokes my face. Kisses my nose. Funny how endearing these small gestures always are. 'Aren't I allowed to have *anything?*'

'Well, that depends what it is. Not me. At least not officially. Oh, come on, Paul. You couldn't expect your mother to say, "Bless you, my children," now could you?'

He releases me. I've depressed him. I sit on the floor at his feet; I have enough self-confidence to enjoy placing myself at an apparent disadvantage. In the right mood I like gazing up at people and listening. The warmth of human contact, I suppose that's really all I want. Corny.

'I was always such a good little boy. So clean and well-behaved. Dear little Paul never had muddy knees or got into fights or had unsuitable friends. Dear little Paul was far too well-bred. The apple of his darling mother's eye, no less.'

He's really bitter. What have I uncovered? 'What about your father?' I hold one of his hands in both mine and stroke it.

'Oh, Dad was an invalid for years before he died. And before that he was always away a lot on business. I – we didn't get a lot of time together, all three of us, I mean, as a family. I was always being presented to him with my latest achievement, like a school report or Oxford entrance. Or I was being kept quiet and out of his way. Oh, my mother must have found me a great comfort. She didn't get quite the life she expected either. Still, which of us does? I shouldn't complain.'

'Complain all you like if it helps.'

'Oh, Alexa . . . You're so good for me.'

'I hope so. Make the most of me, love, if I am, 'cos I won't be here long.'

'No. Oh Christ, what a mess it all is.'

'No, it isn't. It's perfectly all right.'

'But I want – can't I see you in London?'

Smile. Gently, now. 'But you're never *in* London.'

'No. But if I could be – for a conference or something.'

I kiss his hand. Flattery is lovely but this sort makes me feel sad. 'No, love, you couldn't. Not really. Think how complicated it would all be. And after I've gone, you know, you won't even want to, you'll find.'

'Really? That's a guarantee, is it? You're so sure you know how I'll feel.'

'Oh, don't be angry. It's just a lovely few days in a vacuum. We'll both have lovely memories and no harm done.'

'I see. Of course I shouldn't argue with you. You're bound to be right. You've had so much experience, haven't you?'

Oh dear. Knew we'd come to that. 'Paul, what does it matter about my experience? I'm just telling you the way it usually goes.'

'Yes, I see. Meaning I should be grateful for my good, clean-living wife and my lovely home and my two beautiful children. Oh yes. And I am, believe me, I am. But can't you see *anything*? Where's all your great writer's insight? Can't you see how I want you, more than I've ever ...'

All right. Wanted any woman before. (As far as you remember.) 'Well. I'm here now.' It's only novelty. If he gets enough he won't care any more.


He's violent this time. He wants to hurt me. Or maybe just to make an impression in the only way he knows, or the only way he thinks will count with me. Bruising my back on the floorboards under his weight. Trying one thing after another, frantic, desperate.

\*　　　\*　　　\*

'Alexa.'

'Mm.'

'That was fantastic.'

'Mm.'

'Was it all right for you?'

'Couldn't you feel? Or were you too busy to notice?'

'Oh, all right, be like that, damn you. God. You're pretty marvellous, do you know that?'

'I'm glad I meet with your approval.'

'Mm. You're very ... relaxed, aren't you?'

'I suppose so.'

'Alexa, how many men have you had?'

'Oh, Paul.'

'No, really. I want to know.'

'But *I* don't know. Do you think I keep a score or something?'

'I see. You don't want to tell me. Well, that's all right. Serves me right for asking. None of my business. I'm only one more in the long line, after all.'

'It isn't that at all. I just don't think of people as numbers. I'd have to lie here and count – it's not ...' And my back is beginning to hurt.

He gets up, thank God, but angry. We both start to dress. It's really quite cold now : I didn't notice before.

—

## 21

SUNDAY. Grandmother presides. Much talk of Christine. Paul very vocal and animated, playing with children, reminding me pointedly how glad I'll be to get back to London. His eyes steely blue and very cold. I didn't think we were sufficiently involved to have a row. Take refuge in work. Thank God, at last a chance to catch up. Great opportunity with Mrs Davies to see to the kids. I do a huge roast Sunday lunch, all traditional, and retire to my room for an afternoon at the machine. Flattering cries of 'Lexa' from Michael before they distract him. Work quite frantically, time running out. Fingertips burn with the friction, shows how out of practice I am. Amazing as always, though, how much can get done, given a clear run at it. Reappear for grand nursery tea. Mrs D. much happier, having had all her beloveds entirely to herself. Paul excessively charming, teasing, remote, icy-cold. Re-incarcerate self after tea, leave them both to the bed-time routine, wish them joy. Type valiantly on, break nail and curse. More than that, oddly find that I want to weep over it and write letter to Robert. Or phone Erin. Or see my mother. Oh God, I just want to be *home*.

About eight Paul's voice on the stairs. 'I'm just running Mother home. Can you listen out for the kids?' – 'Sure, but isn't she staying for supper?' All cold and ready, my third *tour de force*. At home I shan't cook for a month, I promise myself. 'No. She wants to get back.' Pretty obvious really. 'Okay.' I put my head round the door. No Paul. Mrs Davies at foot of stairs. 'Thank you so much, my dear, for a delightful day.' – 'Not at all, Mrs Davies, I'm grateful to you. I've got such a lot of work done for a change.'

Door bangs. An extraordinary silence settles down on the house, an amazing emptiness. At home I can't work unless alone in the flat; here it seems the reverse. I find that I have to get up, move around, go on a tour of the house as if it were unfamiliar to me. What if this were my life? Eat my cold supper quickly and alone so as not to be eating with Paul later on. Maybe it's not the house and the silent emptiness, maybe I've just done enough for today and I couldn't work any more anywhere. I *have* done a lot. Clever me. Stop in front of hall-stand mirror, where coffee-tray rested, stare at reflection. Time I was moving on.

Michael restless upstairs, cries a bit, calls out. I go up. Dreaming perhaps. Baby sleeps through it all. We have story with pictures and pointing. A queer sort of pang as I read, as for a man you are fond of but do not quite love, or a once-beloved book you've outgrown. A goodnight hug, quite surprisingly tight. Do I deserve it?

I want to telephone someone but do not know whom. And anyway, what to say? I hover over the phone but do not pick it up. Disorientated ... I wander away and the sudden shrill blast makes me jump.

'Hullo.'

'Oh, hullo ... Alexa.'

'*Christine*. How are you, love?' I test my reactions. Do I

feel guilty? No, just keyed up and startled. But excited and genuinely pleased. Relief. I do not want to spoil, even one-sidely, a friendship I value.

'I'm fine. Can I speak to Paul?'

'I'm sorry, he's out. He's driving his mother home.'

'Oh. *She's* been over, has she?'

'Yes, all day.'

'Lucky you.'

'Well, I did get some work done.'

'Oh, good. That's something. Oh, Alexa . . .'

'What, love? Are you okay?'

'Oh yes.' Long sigh. 'Alexa, it's so funny being here. And talking to you on your phone and you on mine.'

'I know. Yes, of course, it must be. But are you enjoying yourself? Have you seen lots of people?'

'Yes, lots and lots.' How odd her voice sounds, little-girl far away. So young and so distant. Breathless. 'I don't know if I love it or hate it.'

'What? What do you mean?'

'I don't know. Everything.' Is it just London that's working on her? 'What would you say if I never came back?'

Laugh. What else?

'Alexa, it's so funny.'

'Are you all right?'

'Oh yes. I've been drinking. I raided your drinks. Well, you did say I could.'

'Yes, of course. Don't be silly.'

'Oh, it's lovely. Everything's lovely. I'm all drunk and there's London . . . But I do miss you all.'

'When will you be home, by the way?'

Long pause. Sigh. 'Oh, I don't know, I don't want to think. Probably Wednesday. But I'll phone again before then.'

'Okay.'

'Alexa, how are Michael and Simon?'

'They're fine.'

'Not playing you up?'

'No, not at all. They've been awfully good.'

'Really? And you're coping all right?'

'Well, I'm muddling through.'

'Is it awful?'

'No. Just exhausting.'

'I know. You see what I mean.'

'Yes, I certainly do.'

Pause. 'And Paul, is he okay?'

'Yes, fine. Valiantly washing his own shirts.'

'Oh, that's good. Well, I suppose I'd better go. Give them all my love or something.'

'Yes. Shall I get him to call you back when he comes in?'

Long pause. 'Well, you could. No, don't. Don't bother. Just tell him I rang.'


22


'CHRISTINE rang.'

'Oh. What did she say?'

'Nothing much. She sounded ... funny.'

'What d'you mean, funny?'

'I don't know. Just odd. She'd been drinking, she said.'

'That's not like Chris.' Disturbed.

'Away from my influence, you mean.'

'Oh, Alexa. Don't be like that.'

I turn over. I'm tired. Confused. 'I wasn't expecting you tonight.'

'I – wanted to apologize.'

'What for?'

'You know perfectly well what for. I've been thoroughly unpleasant to you all day.'

'Not at all. You put on a good display for your mother, just as I suggested. Splendid. I'm awfully tired, Paul; I've done a lot of work and I've had it.'

'Meaning, you want me to go away?'

Oh God. I'm so bad at this. 'Meaning what I say that's all.'

Pause. Resentful, humiliated voice. 'I don't seem able to stay away from you.'

'That's all right.' I'm just no good at this intense bit. Not tonight anyway. He paces around. Smokes. 'Did Chris say when she's coming back?'

'Probably Wednesday. But she said she'd phone again before then.'

'Oh. Only three ... days more then.'

'Mm.' Can I sleep now?

'Alexa, I never meant to do this to Chris. It's – it's the first time. D'you believe me?'

'Of course I do.' Sticks out a mile.

Heavy sad voice. 'I never thought I'd do this to her. Ever.'

'Paul.' Heave myself up in bed reluctantly. Light own cigarette. 'Look, you haven't done anything to her. As long as she doesn't know she won't be hurt. That's all there is to it.'

No reply. More pacing.

'Look, I told you before, from the very beginning. Just don't feel guilty. So long as you haven't hurt her there's nothing to feel guilty about. Honestly.' God, I'm just not equal to morality lessons at this hour.

'I don't mean anything to you, do I?'

'What do you want to mean to me? You love Christine.'

'And you love Robert – do you?'

That's none of your business. 'I'm not married. Robert doesn't come into this.'

Sits on the bed, staring at me. He's actually suffering, I think : going through some intense, tormented *thing*, anyway, and I'm no help at all. 'Will you tell him?'

'I don't know. Maybe. Maybe not.'

'I see. It's that unimportant.'

'Oh, *don't*.' Reach for whisky. 'Do you want a drink?'

'Yes.' Hang-dog. I pour out a glass and we share it.

'Look, love cheer up. You've got Christine and I've got Robert and we've had a lovely time together. Don't spoil it.'

'I see. You mean it's over.'

'Oh, Paul.' Helpless, hopeless. Oh, childhood fantasy, to be magicked away out of all this nonsense on a Persian carpet, floating high over the rooftops, in through my own window, all Nana and Wendy and Peter Pan . . . But Christine's there in my bed. Foiled.

Hand on my arm. Still strangely electric. My hormones or whatever they are must be my worst enemy. 'But she's not coming back till Wednesday.'

'No.' Loaded silence. 'Look, love, if you want to come to bed, come; just don't be guilty and sad, that's all. I can't bear it.'

'Can't you? I shouldn't have thought it would matter a damn to you.'

Oh God. He just doesn't see. In common humanity, I can't bear anyone to be like this if I can prevent it. 'Come on.' Hold out arms. Know I'm a fool.

'Oh, Alexa.' Undressing rapidly. 'I'm sorry I was such a bastard all day.'

'Doesn't matter.' More whisky. 'Just be happy now, or I shall feel a failure.'

'You're anything but that.' Nearly naked. 'You've got it made. You're young and rich and beautiful and talented.' Pale but muscular body, must be games at school. Expect he tans in the summer. 'And I'm just a beggar at the gate. Isn't that about it? Still maybe the beggar can teach the queen a thing or two.' Getting into bed. 'Now then. Where shall we start?'

My bed is suddenly a battle-ground. So that's how he wants it. Making love with controlled hostility. I do believe he actually hates me. Murmuring half-audibly: 'You do want it, don't you? Is this what you want? And this? And this? Go on, tell me. I could kill you, you know. Do you realize that?' Hands on my neck. 'I'm stronger than you and I could kill you. What would you have to say then?'

I'm choking; he's throttling me. Pain in my throat and a blinding light, blurred, my eyes defocusing. But all the time a distant observer remarking, 'Aren't people extraordinary? You never can tell.' Pressure suddenly relaxed, enough for me to say, 'Nothing, I expect. But you'd have a bit of explaining to do.'

'Christine's friend.' Moving in and out of me slowly, exquisitely. 'Christine's dear little friend, her great idol, her favourite person. She wouldn't be so keen on you now if she could see you fucking her husband.' Sudden violent thrust, taking me by surprise. I cry out. 'Ah, that's better. You're going to come for me, aren't you, and come and come till you wish you were dead, till you don't remember you're the great Alexa King sitting in judgment on us lesser mortals. You didn't really want me, did you, but you're going to, by God, you're going to. You're going to want me and I'm going to have you and have you till you beg me to stop but I'm not going to stop. I'm not ever going to stop. This is what you want, isn't it? Well, now you're getting it, and it's going on for ever. I'm going to fuck you for ever. I'm going to make you cry. I'm going to make you bleed.'

Extraordinary. The other times so silent, whether gentle or rough, and now he might be trying to impersonate Robert and he doesn't even know him. Extraordinary. But it works. I do come and it's glorious and who cares if he hates me, though he certainly does. And of course he can't keep it up. After the first two or three times and the look of triumph I love, for he needs it so much, he's as lost as I am, and I have my turn, see his loss of control, see the look, hear the cry, that both cancel out everything, feel or imagine I feel the great rush of glorious juice that I always want to think has magical properties as it might be in some unwritten adult fairy tale, a charmed potion indeed, and he comes and it's over.

'Alexa.'

'Paul.'

Our two names out of an immense silence filled only with breathing as our hearts settle down. No wonder they thought that it shortened your life. And what of it? The usual great tide of friendship and well-being, that seems, now the pleasure is over, the only possible reason for such an upheaval. And the usual lack : a word compounded of liking and love and retrospective satisfied lust and the most intense kind of pure, transitory kinship. Nothing to say. We stroke each other. Kiss, look for ever into each other's eyes. Dumb. And the longer the better. Words, when you come to them, only float you away, back to harbour, back to reality. With every word you put distance between yourself and the recurrent illusion of immortality. And yet the only possible time to talk, to communicate, to say real things. All barriers down. If only he could stay in me for ever. So often you find that masquerading lust is really just loneliness and a yearning to be one again and not half. Such a cruel joke of the gods.

'That's what it should always be like.'
'I know. Well, it was.'
Smiling at each other with infinite good-will.
'You're wonderful.'
'So are you.'
Contentment spilling out of us. We've worked the miracle again for each other.
'That's all it's about.'
'Yes, I know.'
'Only it gets covered up.'
'Never mind. It's still there underneath. And we've had it. It can't be wiped out. It's there to remember whenever we want it.' Warm, virtuous feeling of ultimate benefit given and received. Like friendship and work : triple peaks of achievement. The creation of more where before there was less.
'I've always felt such a failure.'
'Well, now you know better.'
'I don't mean just in bed. In work and everything. As a person. But you take me up to the sky.'
'That's a lovely thing to say.' That too is a reason for doing it, to catch little gifts like that. 'You see? That's all it's about, making each other feel good.'

Next door, incredibly, for it seems so remote, a child cries. The outside world, breaking in already. Trust the gods to remind us so soon that we're only mortal. For in bed my tailor-made, custom-built deity fades and I become pagan again.

'I'd better go.'
'Okay. But come back to sleep.'
Completely relaxed, without stress. The only way to exist. I did not believe it when the front door opened and closed. I lay there and listened to the simple, unmistakable sound and did not believe it. Footsteps downstairs in the hall, and

my body acted for me, getting out of bed, closing my door very quietly, putting out the light. I stood in the dark in the middle of the room and listened and did not believe. But I knew it was true.

Paul called out from the nursery, 'Who's that?' And Christine's voice replied, floating up the stairs, reaching both of us, 'It's me, love. I'm back.'

## 23

'I JUST couldn't bear it a minute longer,' she said at breakfast. 'After I phoned you I just sat there and thought about you all, and the children asleep, and I just couldn't bear it, I had to come back.'

'Well, of course,' I said. 'It's great to see you. But you did enjoy it while you were there?'

'Oh yes,' she said rapturously. 'Yes.' But she closed her eyes; she looked more tired than I felt. 'You can't go back though. I think I knew that really. Oh, God, Alexa, it's not a very original conclusion, is it?'

Michael, playing in a corner of the kitchen near Simon's high chair, eyes us both sullenly; he had been fractious since his mother's return. I felt immensely at one with Christine, nothing to do with Paul, yet not cancelling anything, though proving perhaps that friendship is stronger than sex, hence the proverbial power of love.

'No,' I said. 'But I know how you feel. I must go back.'

She sat on a stool and looked at me. Her eyes were a little red, whether from tears or lack of sleep; there were shadows under them that made her look older. I loved her. I wanted to put my arms round her and hug her and comfort her. I wished we could all say the truth to each other in safety, without fear. I envied my parents, and I held my tongue.

'You belong there,' she said, 'and I don't. But I wish I did. Oh God—'. She looked round the room as if for witnesses – 'You'll never know how much.'

'Any time,' I said. 'Any time. You know that, don't you? Any time you want to, just ring up and come. Let Paul—' It was good to get his name spoken and out of the way – 'or his mother look after the kids. And if I'm away, my mother or Erin will have a key.'

'Away,' she said vaguely. 'You're going away?'

'I'm not sure yet,' I said. 'But Robert wants me to join him in the States, meet his parents, that kind of thing. I don't know yet; I haven't answered his letter.'

'So that's going well,' she said warmly. 'I'm glad.'

I laughed. 'Now don't get that matchmaking look in your eyes. It's not that kind of visit.'

'Oh, really?' she said. 'What kind of visit then?'

'Just a visit.' But I did rather yearn, I had to admit, for Robert : for his coolness and irony and warmth, for his insight and strength. For the way he would see through me and accept me. There are times when I think there is only one brand to be stamped on our relationship : *warts and all.* Not very elegant, perhaps, but realistic.

'America,' she said. 'What fun.' And for a moment I thought she was going to cry. But she covered her face with her hand and then went on gaily, 'You know, I was crazy to come back last night. I only just caught the last train out of town and then I had to get a minicab from the station. It cost me the earth.'

'Why didn't you phone?' I said. 'You could have got Paul to fetch you.'

'Oh no,' she said. 'It was so late by then. I didn't want to wake the whole house. Especially these two monsters.' She patted the baby and Michael, who moved away and pointedly played with a toy. 'And now, of course,' she said resignedly, 'he's taking it out on me for going away. Oh well, he'll get over it.'

'So long as you enjoyed yourself,' I said. 'That's all. I do hope you did.'

'Oh, I did,' she said. 'I really did. It's just too late – you know.'

'I know.'

'I didn't realize,' she said, 'how you can belong somewhere you don't want to be. It's a funny thing, that. It's got nothing to do with what you want. And I didn't realize how long ago it all was. Oh, well.' She looked at her hands. 'D'you know, I actually went to a concert, for the first time in years. Bach and Chopin at the Festival Hall.' She smiled, a trifle lop-sidedly. 'That really did it. Anyway. It was lovely and here I am. Back. How are you? You look tired.'

I managed a smile of my own. 'I'm afraid,' I said, 'that I never quite grasped one essential point : that early mornings are not compatible with late nights.' She laughed. 'I did all my typing at night and the six o'clock good-morning campers took me quite by surprise, every time.'

'I know,' she said. 'It is a bit like that.'

'But the children were marvellous,' I went on. 'Once I got used to them. Really. They were no trouble at all, I enjoyed them. And Paul and his mother did masses to help. I was awfully spoilt.' I still felt a trifle odd with her : not guilty at all but sad that I had to conceal from her something of which I was not ashamed. The way I suppose I might have felt about Robert, towards a more conventional mother : an artificial barrier, an area of non-communication with someone you love. The trouble with me was, I thought, that there was far too much room in my heart.

She smiled. 'It's funny,' she said, 'isn't it? Like changing lives. Like the Prince and the Pauper.'

'Hardly like that,' I said. 'But I know what you mean.'

She looked at me straight but with marvellous gentleness. 'Yes,' she said. 'I thought you would. Do be careful, won't you?'

I felt a faint chill. 'What do you mean?' But I misunderstood; I was not expecting generosity.

'Don't let it happen to you,' she said, 'not too soon. Not till you're really ready. Not till you know what it means.'

## 24

Darling Mother,

What the hell are you doing still in Paris with Giovanni? A post-card is all very well and it helps to know the name of your hotel, but I've still a good mind to send hourly telegrams along the lines of Mother, come home, all is forgiven, in ten different languages. (If I knew ten different languages.) After all I've been back for a week, which means you've had nearly a fortnight. Don't you realize your children *need* you?

Actually, if you don't come back soon we may cross in the post, as it were, as I may be joining Robert in America. He's not coming back in the immediate future and is getting quite pressing for me to meet his elusive parents. The more I hear about them, the more I marvel that they ever got together long enough to produce Robert. So I'd like to observe them in action and America would be fun and I might – who knows? – get a book out of it and be able to claim it on tax. Besides – yes, all right – it does seem a while since Robert and I were together. And you can take that how you like. I'll be only too delighted if it panics you into returning, and you can tell Giovanni I didn't think much of his last film – no, actually, I did, but he's conceited enough already.

But seriously, as they say, I would like to talk to you; I can't write such beautiful letters as you and it's not fair to force me to try. I finally got the articles done and in the post, so I feel very virtuous. I put on a real sprint as soon as I got back and worked day and night between intervals of slipping out to see people. I even saw Maria, who doesn't seem to have broken anything recently and who told me with tears in her eyes about the good home you have found for her and her future bambino with "the lovely Mrs Gould." Poor Erin. What *are* we doing to her? She'll be praying for Ingrid again in a week, boyfriends and measles and all. But you've had a lucky escape. Just see it doesn't happen again, that's all, because I haven't any more friends with such abnormally soft hearts.

Essex seems a lifetime ago, or a million light-years, or something. Paul and I had, as you probably guessed, what is probably called a mini-affair. I hope I did him some good. He seemed plagued by guilt, which was rather a pity, but there were some lovely moments nevertheless. He suffers from a sense of failure : academic, financial, and sexual, and seems overwhelmed by Christine's maternal drive, and a little resentful that he didn't pack more bad girls like me into his lost youth. All rather sad. I don't know what he was more jealous of, really : my apparent success as a writer, my freedom or my friendship with Christine. I seemed to be a challenge and a reproach to him at every turn, putting rather a hostile edge on our relationship. But it all worked out. We had a near miss, though, or a lucky escape : Christine came back unexpectedly in the middle of the night, but thank God, he was up with one of the children, so that was all right. Ideal, really. I didn't see him again as I left the next day. He wasn't very good at putting on a front for his mother so I didn't want to test him with Christine. I must admit it wasn't a situation I wanted to get into, but there it is : it happened, it's over and no harm done – I hope positive good. At least Christine got a few days holiday and Paul boosted his ego. I think they were both ripe for a change and I answered their needs very well. Their marriage is at a kind of grey in-between stage but they obviously love each other a lot. Whether they would have been happier married to two other people is, of course, another matter; it's so hard to judge what is temperament, and what money, and what day to day strain. It all made me think quite a lot but not very constructively, I'm afraid, and always returning to the same fixed point : how exceptionally lucky you and Daddy were. They are both, I think, missing the sort of intensity they used to have and they don't know how to get it back. For Christine it seems to be in motherhood now instead of music, and for Paul, well, I suppose I answered some need, though he really wants

Christine as she used to be. They both seem oppressed by a lack of drama in their lives, which only confirms everything you've always said about marriage, though not everyone is so able to find a solution, and the right kind of partner. All very sobering really. I shall die a spinster yet.

Anyway, love, that's about it, at least all I can bother to write, though if you were here I should talk you into the ground and exhaust you with detail. Essex really is the end of the world, you were quite right as usual, and it's great to be back among the living. Now I've got the work over I shall endeavour to make myself sick with a surfeit of parties, people, clothes, books, films, food, before I leave for the jungle of New York and Hollywood. Who knows? Some misguided producer may even offer me a script. But come back soon regardless. I want to feast my eyes on you before I go.

Love as always,
Alexa.

(*Posted, unluckily, one day too soon.*)

## 25

THE telegram took me quite by surprise. I realize, of course, that this is what telegrams are supposed to do, but this one seemed peculiarly startling, in that it was pushed through my door while I was out, not delivered in person by a postman eager for an answer and a tip. I only just noticed it, too, as I returned with my arms full of parcels and no reason to inspect the carpet at my feet for a small yellow envelope. I dumped everything and picked it up, feeling quite cheerful and confident, as I always assume telegrams are to do with work and congratulation : bad news, if any, comes on the phone. I opened it, expecting I don't know what but definitely something pleasant, and there it was in that peculiarly pale, clear type on the stuck-on white strips they always use, surely designed to take the emotion out of anything.

## CHRISTINE IN HOSPITAL SUICIDE ATTEMPT. PAUL.

I swear I had to read this twice before it meant anything. The first time I read it I had no reaction at all : the words did not connect. It might have been any kind of message. The second time it burst upon me like a physical shock, as from a wave of cold water or a searchlight shone suddenly in my eyes. I was blinded, frozen, stunned.

I found myself at the phone and rang their number as soon as I could bring myself to remember it. As it rang I tried to make my brain work. I had no idea what I was going to say, but as soon as someone answered I should have to speak. It went on ringing and I began to feel a mixture of relief and despair at the unexpected delay. A reprieve – if only I could make use of it. But my brain remained obstinately numb. Finally, as the ringing went on, such a lonely, repetitive sound, anticlimax took over. There was not going to be a reply.

I put down the phone and lit a cigarette. The telegram was still in my hand and I found myself reading it over and over with hideous fascination. So few words. Deprived of action through the telephone, I switched to the verge of hysteria. The words said so little : what had Christine *done*? My mind flew to hideous pictures : blood, gas, pills. What method had she chosen? Was she all right, was that what *attempt* meant, or was there still danger? She could not – she must be all right, they had saved her – surely she could not still ... die? Death was not something I thought about very often. It had only touched me once, when my father died, and he had been no longer young. Even so, the world had never been so bright again and I had merely become accustomed, over the years, to its lesser brilliance. But Christine was my own age, Christine was my friend. She *could* not die. And if she did? Then I would have murdered her.

It was at this point, just as I was about to succumb to

total melodrama, that something clicked in my brain. I had assumed, from the very first moment, that I was responsible, that Christine had attempted suicide because of me. But she *could not* have found out just like that; it was impossible that she could have guessed. There had been nothing in my behaviour, no evidence left behind. I had even used a towel in my bed to protect the sheets, and brought it home with me. I had never been into the room that they shared. And Michael had never seen us embrace. There was not the smallest clue anywhere. So it followed that Paul must have given himself away.

I became angry. Angry as I ordered a mini-cab, (regretting that my own private economy is not even to know how to drive because I maintain that a car is a pointless extravagance in London). Angry as I got into it and began the long journey to Essex. A train might in fact have been quicker but I was incapable of the action involved in checking on trains, and the changes of transport. I needed the anger : I needed anything I could find to replace the sick helplessness of total responsibility. But I thought – insofar as I could think at all – that it was also justified. I had not acted alone. The ties of marriage were presumably as sacred as those of friendship, if we were reduced to using the criteria of society. If Christine had caught us in bed we would both have been equally guilty (though if Paul had not forgotten to put the catch on the door there would have been no chance of her doing so – how these petty details conspire). But she had not caught us. She had known nothing. So whatever she knew now, whatever she had discovered, to bring her to this, she had found out through Paul. A totally avoidable discovery. My anger mounted. And having done this much damage he had not even seen fit to warn me. He had chosen to leave me in complete ignorance until this calamity, and for this he had not even telephoned – unless when I was out. (Again the pettiness of everyday facts.) He had sent a telegram.

But it was a long journey to Essex. My anger began to fade even before I recognized it for what it was, my anger, and Paul's telegram : the frantic shuffling of guilty conspirators all desperately passing the blame to and fro like the time-bomb it was. I was not used to guilt; I hated it. I had not until this moment done anything that I considered wrong. Intrinsically, I thought, my actions had been for the best in a difficult situation, and I had not foreseen any necessity for consequences, accustomed as I was to actions that lead precisely to nowhere but are complete in themselves. And I resented being made to feel retrospectively ashamed. I had stepped out of my world and for this I was now being punished.

## 26

I WENT to the house. I did not know where else to go but as I paid off the driver I asked him to wait for a moment in case no one was in. I pictured a crazy tour of all the hospitals in the area until I found the one containing Christine. But the door was eventually opened, and I waved the car away.

Paul said, 'You,' and stood there, looking past me. He seemed shrunken : shorter and thinner, and pale with the pallor of death. He seemed a stranger. And yet at the same time there was the familiarity, curiously akin to blood relationship, that anyone I have ever made love with always acquires for me, to a greater or lesser degree. I wanted to embrace him, to comfort him, to tell him he did not have to bear this alone. His words caught me in this peculiar unbalance.

'How dare you come?' He was still looking over my shoulder down the path, as if I were not really there. 'How do you have the nerve to come here again?' His voice was very flat and quite without emotion. I was shocked.

'I got your telegram,' I said. 'I telephoned and nobody answered. What did you expect me to do?'

'I was at the hospital,' he said. When I looked at him more closely I saw that his eyes were puffy and blood-shot. 'I went to see her.' Still he looked out at the road where the traffic passed ; still we stood on the step.

I said, 'May I come in?' and at that he began to tremble violently.

'No,' he said. 'I don't think so.' His voice now suddenly shaking as much as his body. 'I'd rather you never set foot in this house again. And I wish to God you never had.'

There was a little breeze blowing; I had not noticed it before. Now it lifted my hair and blew strands across my face. I pushed them away.

'I wish to God I'd never set eyes on you,' he said. He began to weep; he put his face in his hands and muffled the great tearing sobs.

I said gently, 'How is she? Just tell me that, please.'

He made a choking sound that was almost a laugh. He wiped his eyes savagely and took his hands from his face. 'Why?' he said. 'Why should you care? *You.*' He looked at me with such hatred that I was alarmed.

'Look,' I said, feeling at a terrible disadvantage, poised on the step and receiving the full blast of his distress. 'I'm sorry you feel like that but we're in this together. I'm as worried as you.'

'That's a laugh,' he said. 'That really is a laugh. You've never been worried about anyone except yourself in the whole of your life.'

It hardly seemed the moment to defend my character. I said patiently, 'Just tell me how she is.'

He hesitated for a moment before coming out with the word. 'Alive,' he said, and choked. He produced a handkerchief from somewhere and used it. 'Oh God,' he said eventually. 'You'd better come in, I suppose.'

I went in quickly before he could change his mind and he closed the door. There was a lot more that I wanted to know. I said soothingly, 'Shall I make some coffee? I'm sure we both need some,' but he jumped as if I had struck him and said, 'Don't touch anything. Anything. Just stay where you are.' Then he sagged against the wall as if his legs would no longer support him. I had never seen anyone whose emotional state showed itself in such acutely physical terms.

I said, 'Paul, you must tell me what happened. Please.' And he looked up sharply.

'Oh, of course you must know all the details,' he said. 'After all, they might come in useful.'

'That's not fair,' I said, before I could stop myself. 'I'm involved. For God's sake. You're not alone in this.'

'Aren't I?' he said. 'Aren't I indeed?'

I waited, but he said no more; I thought we had come to another impasse. Then he said, 'Well, for the record. Are you listening? Don't miss anything now. She – swallowed a bottle of pills. I – just couldn't wake her. This morning she – just didn't wake. And I thought she was dead.' He turned on me savagely. 'Can you think what that means? No, of course you can't. To wake up and see her lying there beside me and think she was dead. They had to pump out her stomach.' He turned his face to the wall. Presently he said, 'I never realized how much I love her.'

Well that, I thought, was something. Something positive at any rate. 'And she's going to be all right?'

He didn't answer at once. Finally he said, 'So they say. Oh God, so they say. But it would be all the same if she wasn't. We'd have killed her, you and I. That's what we did.'

I was not sure how much accusation I could take even out of respect for his grief. 'There's one other thing,' I said. 'Just tell me this and I'll go. How did she find out?'

He stared at me as if I were mad. 'I told her, of course,' he said. 'I confessed.'

A very cold anger, much stronger than that in the car, now I knew that Christine was all right, began to creep over me. I almost shivered with it. I said very clearly, 'What the hell for?'

He seemed surprised : he said with a kind of mild, blank amazement, 'Because I had to, that's why. What else could I do?'

'Because she suspected?' I prompted.

'No. No, she had no idea.'

'That's what I thought.' I found I was clenching my fists; my nails hurt. I found myself longing to do him some violent injury. 'She had no idea and you just had to tell her. Well, pardon me for being so dense but *what the hell for?*'

I began to see how people got themselves knifed; it was as well for Paul that I had no offensive weapon.

He still looked amazed but now hostile as well. 'Because I felt unclean,' he said. I could see him measuring the effect of his words as he chose them. 'I felt dirty all over. I wasn't fit to sleep next to her. I wasn't fit to touch her.' All this was accompanied by a look that suggested I was something from under a stone. I remembered my arrival, my best of intentions; I remembered Christine urging us to drive to the beach, insisting on her holiday, leaving us alone. I remembered Paul's urgency and my reluctance. I remembered my repeated warnings. All this passed through my mind and something began to tick ominously at the back of it.

'I see,' I said. I was frightened of my own cold rage. 'You felt unclean so you had to confess. For what? So she could forgive you?'

'She took it very well,' he said, dreamily. 'She said it didn't matter.'

I wondered if this had somehow disappointed him. Never mind. He had been amply rewarded by the tablets.

'So you simply told her,' I went on, 'to make yourself feel better. And you say you love her. Well, pray God I never run into that kind of love.'

'You don't understand,' he said, seeming quite hurt. 'It wasn't like that. We couldn't go on with that thing between us. It was like a horrible shadow poisoning everything.'

I hate it when amateurs use imagery in everyday speech. Perhaps I let my distaste show in my face for he said, 'But you wouldn't understand that. What do you know about love?'

I had had enough. I braced myself for finale and departure. 'Nothing,' I said. 'Absolutely nothing. If love is telling someone something that you know will hurt them, if you do that to make yourself feel better because you can't bear to put up with your own guilt alone, then you're right. I don't know about love, and I don't want to know.'

He just went on looking at me with the same disgust, only now it was mutual. 'You don't understand,' he said. 'It was the only thing I could do. It had to be done.' There was a peculiar finality in his words and a sort of veiled import which I then had no time to consider.

'Which hospital?' I said casually.

'What?'

'Which hospital is she in?'

'Oh, you can't see her,' he said instantly. 'She's not allowed visitors. Except me—' And I wondered if I was imagining the trace of smugness. 'Besides—'

'Oh, quite,' I said briskly. 'It would be in very bad taste, would it not? I just wanted to send her some flowers. Am I allowed to do that?'

He told me. I opened the door for myself and he closed it behind me; we did not speak another word. I walked down the path to the road and stopped to consider my plans : I found I was trembling all over and not just from anger. I really do hate any relationship, however brief, that ever meant anything, that was ever good, to end so badly. It's a very special kind of indecency and should not be possible.

27

FINDING the hospital was easy. I simply stood in the path of an oncoming car and flagged it down with dramatic gestures. The word hospital worked total magic, melting all indignation and surprise. But once there, getting in was another matter and required considerable ingenuity. I could not afford to be seen and rejected; my first visit would of necessity be my last. So after a little thought I walked down the road to a phone box and got as much information as I could under pretext of relationship. I was told quite sternly that only Mr Davies was allowed to visit but I did at least discover Christine's whereabouts, to which to send flowers and messages, in considerable detail, even down to the number of her private room. I must have been lucky and got hold of a slightly dim or unusually compliant nurse – or perhaps a ward-aide, for whom they are always advertising, and who was uncertain how much information must not be divulged.

Thus armed, I walked back and in, before courage failed me. I had long ago learned, in a variety of situations, that if you appear nonchalant and purposeful and full of a right to be wherever you are, it is unlikely that anyone will question you. Moreover, if you walk briskly along in a place where people are busy, the odds are they will not take time to stop you and question you. All the same, it would be dishonest to pretend that my tour of the hospital corridors, exuding this kind of false confidence, did not cause me considerable unease. I had to keep reminding myself, as I tried unobtrusively to get my bearings, that hospitals are frequented by all kinds of people, not merely visitors but therapists, lecturers, students and out-patients, and I could be any one of these. As long as I did not hesitate and look lost, I should probably get through. And I also clung to my slightly fatalistic belief that in cases of sufficient need, the gods weight the dice in your favour.

As it happened, I did get through, though it all appeared at first a rather nasty maze and at one point I became less concerned with getting through and more concerned with getting out, for it seemed to me very easy to go on walking these corridors for ever. When at last I did find the room it came almost as a surprise and not entirely a pleasant one. I wanted, quite frankly, to run away. For it is one thing to conceive a plan such as this, quite another to carry it out. But the room was near a convenient loo (the work of the biased gods, this) into which I dodged till the corridor was empty. And then it was the work of a moment, as they say in a certain type of adventure story, to slip into the room itself.

Christine was asleep. She looked very small and pale, and the room was banked high with flowers; it was like visiting someone in a miniature Kew. I stood there and looked at her, and despite the suspicions I had formed (Lucas, too, had been a dab hand at attempted suicide in her time, with gratifying effect) my heart did a kind of lurch which I took to mean pity and love. I now had to attract her attention – well, to wake her up – and I pondered this problem. I did not feel I could shake her by the shoulder, nor did it seem appropriate to stand there genteely clearing my throat, as if demanding service in a shop. So I just said, 'Christine', very softly, and then louder and louder, with a panic sense that time at any moment could run out on me. And at last she opened her eyes.

'You,' she said, just like Paul.

'Yes, me.' I stood at the foot of the bed. 'I hope you don't mind but I just had to see you.'

She made an odd sound, somewhere between a moan and a giggle. 'I knew you'd come,' she said. 'I was waiting for you.'

I was pleased. I don't know what I had expected – perhaps violent abuse or hysteria; I had not allowed myself to anticipate my reception in case I dared not come at all. But there was something comforting about Christine's certain foreknowledge, a certain satisfaction in playing a pre-ordained role. Nevertheless I was still, while wildly hoping all might yet be well, remarkably lost for words.

'Now I'm here,' I said feebly, 'I don't know what to say. And there's so much I ought to say.' I swallowed. 'Look, love—'

But she cut me short. 'I don't know either.' She looked very small and somehow hunched up in the high hospital bed, like a child, pale from incarceration and the aftermath of some infectious disease. 'It's funny, isn't it?'

And at that moment I realized that it actually was, though I would never myself have dared to select such a word. We looked at each other, and very nearly, very briefly – well, for a second I was sure that we were both actually going to laugh, as in the old days, as about Jenkins or Paul's mother or some other piece of shared cynicism. Then Christine said quietly, 'Are you very angry with me?'

The question was so unexpected that for a moment it deprived me of speech. Finally I managed to say, 'God, I thought it was meant to be the other way round.'

'Oh, it was,' she said dreamily. 'It was. I think. I'm awfully woozy, Alexa; I don't know what they've done to me.'

The use of my name was totally disarming. I moved

round the bed, desperately needing contact with her, and she put out her hand at once. We clasped hands. In a way it was the most intense moment of my life.

'How funny,' she said. 'It's just the same. Only more so. And I thought I'd hate you. No. I didn't know how I'd feel till I saw you. But I wanted to know.'

We went on holding hands. I sat on the edge of the bed and stroked her thin wrist. I said, 'It seems totally inadequate, love, to say how sorry I am, God, I've been demented since I got the telegram ...'

Again she interrupted me. 'Oh,' she said. 'He sent you a telegram, did he?'

'Yes.'

She nodded, seeming satisfied. 'Yes,' she said. 'He would. They're very dramatic, telegrams.'

I burst out, suddenly beyond myself : 'I don't see why he had to tell you. God knows I'm not trying to make excuses for myself, believe me, but for Christ's sake, why, why the hell did he have to tell you anything?' I felt my eyes stinging and wished I could allow myself to cry, but it would have seemed too blatant a bid for sympathy where none was deserved and too much had already been given.

'Oh,' she said, with a sort of old, wise serenity. 'He had to. There was nothing else he could do.'

She was using the same fatalistic tone that Paul himself had used; it struck me very forcibly. I said, 'D'you mean it was actually necessary in some way?'

She took her hand away, but not in a hostile way, merely pushing back a piece of hair with it, then letting it fall back on the sheet. 'I think so,' she said softly. And then : 'Oh dear, I am a dishonest cow. You know? It's like that thing about your left hand and your right hand not knowing – God, I'm so woozy – I was doing things and not looking at what I was doing, just doing it and looking later, when it was all over. Alexa—' and she tried to half-raise herself on her pillows – 'd'you ever sleep walk?'

I said, 'No, but go on.'

'Well, it was like that, I imagine. I mean I don't sleep walk either so I'm not sure. But I think I was in a kind of trance.'

I said desperately, 'Christine, what *are* you trying to tell me?'

'Slowly,' she said. 'It takes time. I'm not really conscious, you know.'

I lit a cigarette. I could feel my nerves tingling and snapping in that nasty way they had. I was too far gone even to ask Christine if she minded about the smoke.

'Anyone else,' she said presently, smiling a little, 'and it wouldn't have happened.'

I stared at her. 'Are you saying you wanted it to?' I could hardly get the words out, but once said they seemed quite natural.

'Oh no,' she said. 'I was jealous as hell when it did. Really. Oh, you mightn't think so to look at me now but I was. Great black waves of it, all red hot. Well, something like that. I even wanted to kill you, I think. I kept picturing ... Or maybe just mutilate you a little.' She smiled at what was presumably a look of alarm on my face. 'I felt really violent. That's when I took the tablets.'

I leaned forward. I said urgently, 'Christine, when you took them, did you really want to die? You couldn't, surely, not because of me and Paul. You must have known it didn't mean anything.'

'It had to be you,' she said, and giggled slightly, 'No one else would have done. I knew Paul couldn't resist you and I knew you couldn't resist anyone as desperate as Paul. You see? I know you both so well. I took advantage, didn't I?' And she managed somehow to look both guilty and sad, as well as decidedly pleased with herself.

I said, 'You mean you *planned* it ...'

'Oh no, no ...' She waved her hands vaguely, her stubby, ruined pianist's hands. 'That's much too definite. I didn't think, you see, I just acted. But I made it possible. You were just what Paul needed.'

'And you?'

'Oh, me,' she said vaguely.

'What did you need?'

'I didn't think about that.'

'Well, I'm asking you. Try to think now. Heavens, love, this is serious. You might have died.'

'Yes,' she said with evident pride. 'I might have died. But if you can't go to life, it must come to you.'

'Life,' I said, 'or death. Which? Oh, *think*, Christine, do. What did you really want?'

She smiled; she squeezed my hand again. 'I wanted something to happen.'

There was a pause while I digested this. I even let my thoughts stray far enough to wonder if this was why Tony had stabbed me. It was all very well, all fine words and philosophy, but I could not escape the physical facts of each case: the blood, the stomach pump. I said, 'How many tablets did you take?' but she shook her head.

'I don't know,' she said. 'Quite a lot.'

'But enough?' I insisted.

She smiled. 'I don't know,' she said, again. 'I thought I might die, really I did. But I don't know if I meant to or wanted to. After all,' she added in a very matter-of-fact voice, 'who is ever really honest with themselves?'

I said, 'Probably me, for what it's worth.'

She sighed. 'Yes, probably you. But me, you see, I'm devious.'

'Yes,' I said. 'That's a fair assessment.'

A lovely grin spread over her face. 'Oh God,' she said with surprising energy for an invalid. 'Isn't it wonderful that we can still be friends? It was such a gamble. I was so afraid I'd be too jealous when it came to the point, or you'd be too angry at being used.'

'That's all right,' I said. 'I'm used to it.' And we became hysterical.

'But you mustn't think,' she went on, when she had finished wiping her eyes, 'that I don't take Paul and me seriously. Because I do.'

'Oh yes,' I said. 'I believe you.'

'It's just that—' But she paused and let it go. 'Oh, I'm such a mess. D'you know, I lay here and actually wondered if I was going mad and whether I'd ever know if I did. I mean, how would one tell?'

'Oh, quite,' I said. 'Quite.'

There was a pause after this in which we both looked round nervously as if suddenly aware that we could at any moment be interrupted. I even wondered if it would be more prudent to dive under the bed, now, at once, before a nurse came in. To conduct this particular conversation on two different levels might even be rather appropriate.

'The thing is,' Christine said abruptly, 'Paul must never know.' She stared at me with peculiar intensity. 'Alexa. Do you promise?'

I stared back. I half-wanted to say, 'Paul must never know *what?*' but I understood that she neither could nor would be more explicit than she had been already and to attempt to force her would be less than friendship. So I said simply, 'Yes. I promise.'

She sighed with satisfaction and lay back on her pillows, at peace. In a way it was like a death-bed scene, except that Christine, thank God, was very much alive : more so, in fact, than she had been for a long time. But the atmosphere of solemn assurance was the same.

'I knew you would,' she said, and then. 'Oh, God,' with sudden frenzied energy. 'I wish we had more time. I'm waking up a bit; there's so much I want to say but there isn't time. They'll come and throw you out any minute.'

I said, 'Yes, I know. I keep thinking that myself.'

'I'll write,' she said. 'Oh, I know what I'm like but I really will, now. It's the least I can do. Only – you won't be able to write back. Because he'd never understand and I couldn't explain. It would ruin everything. He has to think this is the end.'

I had not thought this far ahead but I saw it as soon as she said it, clear and nasty and inevitable. 'I know,' I said. 'Maybe I could phone. In the day-time. Or get Lucas to address the envelopes. Or something.'

'Yes,' she said, with curiously childish passion. 'Oh yes. We'll think of something. We'll get round it somehow.' And then the energy went out of her and she slumped again. 'Oh God,' she said. 'I'm sorry. I didn't want to sacrifice you but I didn't have a choice.'

I said gently, 'I know that. I understand.'

'You see, it was grey,' she said. 'In spite of all the love. In spite of everything. And *now* it's vivid again. That's all.'

There were footsteps in the corridor and a rustle of starch; we both quivered with panic. I stood up.

'I didn't have a choice,' she said again, her eyes full of tears, and I took her hand and kissed it, a second before the door opened. The indignation of the nurse surged around us, like the protests of children, disruptive and ignored. Christine said, 'Alexa. Oh, Alexa,' and I said, 'Yes, love. *Love*. It's *okay*. And it *will* be okay. Promise.' And she made a sound that could only be written as 'Mmm' but was in fact the antithesis of the assenting sound that Paul and his mother made: it was a long, shaky whimper of love and sorrow that racked my heart. And then I was hustled out.

## 28

OUR furtive correspondence pursued an erratic life of its own. Sometimes letters were exchanged quite frequently under a variety of cunning disguises on my part, of which I felt quite proud; then there would be long silences during which I tried to calm my vague disquiet with the instinctive certainty that we could never lose touch for ever: we had been too close for that. And my own life absorbed me once again, comforting and disturbing at the same time.

Sometimes Christine wrote freely, as in the old days, as if we were together alone in a room, just talking, late at night. I valued those letters and kept them. The others, brief and stilted, nervously distant and polite, as from a pen-friend in another country, I destroyed: they were invalid and did not count. Then followed a long gap in which I heard nothing in response to anything I wrote. It lasted about six months and half-way through I gave up, unable to sustain such a one-sided enterprise. But I was still confident there would be more to follow. I waited. Sometimes I even knew what I was waiting for. Yesterday it came: the birthday, weight and sex of Pauline Mary, whose arrival

Paul and Christine Davies were proud to announce, on a printed card. At the top Christine had written : 'Forgive me. I didn't know how to tell you.' And at the bottom, in an afterthought scrawl : 'I wish I could have called her Alexa.'

## MORE ABOUT PENGUINS
## AND PELICANS

*Penguinews*, which appears every month, contains details of all the new books issued by Penguins as they are published. From time to time it is supplemented by *Penguins in Print*, which is our complete list of almost 5,000 titles.

A specimen copy of *Penguinews* will be sent to you free on request. Please write to Dept EP, Penguin Books Ltd, Harmondsworth, Middlesex, for your copy.

*In the U.S.A.*: For a complete list of books available from Penguins in the United States write to Dept CS, Penguin Books, 625 Madison Avenue, New York, New York 10022.

*In Canada*: For a complete list of books available from Penguins in Canada write to Penguin Books Canada Ltd, 41 Steelcase Road West, Markham, Ontario.